Confessions, Lies, and Secrets

by

Stu Milisci

Confessions, Lies, and Secrets
by
Stu Milisci

All Rights Reserved
by Stu Milisci Copyright 2015

No part of this book may be reproduced or transmitted in any form or by any means, electronic or mechanical, including photocopying, recording, or by information storage and retrieval system except by a reviewer who may quote brief passages in a review to be printed in a magazine or newspaper, without written permission from the publisher and the author.

This book is a work of fiction. Names, characters, and incidents either are products of the author's imagination or are used fictitiously. Any resemblance to actual events or persons, living or dead, is entirely coincidental.

ISBN 13: 978 1518658983 (Paperback)
ISBN 10: 1518658989 (Paperback)
ASIN: B017AUJG02 (ebook)
Printed in the United States of America

ACKNOWLEDGEMENTS

First and foremost, I would like to thank my wife, Maria, for her patience and support while this book was being written. She read every chapter and provided thoughtful insight and assistance in improving this work. I am forever grateful to her for being my partner and best friend for over fifty years.

Much credit for my endeavor to write a novel goes to my friend and author, Marshall Frank. Marshall has written and published several books and has become a mentor and inspiration. I thank him for taking time to share his wisdom and experience.

Patrick Pesce is a long time friend who joined the NYPD with me almost fifty years ago. He deserves credit for providing his assistance. Pat is a published author who has offered countless hours teaching me how to navigate the Internet and use the computer in general. I am grateful for his unselfish time and dedication to my project.

I would also thank the wonderful Jesuit Priests who educated me as a young man, without whom this book could not have been written.

Confessions, Lies, and Secrets *Stu Milisci*

Father, forgive them. For they know not what *they do.*
Luke 23:34

Things are not always what they seem.
Phaedrus

Confessions, Lies, and Secrets   *Stu Milisci*

CONTENTS

1. Prologue
2. Childhood
3. The Calling
4. The Mean Streets
5. World War II
6. The School
7. Baiting The Hook
8. Hooking The Fish
9. Guilt and Forgiveness
10. The Confrontation
11. The Detective
12. The Rookie
13. The Crime Scene
14. Suspicion
15. The Investigation
16. The Evidence
17. More Evidence
18. The District Attorney
19. The Interviews
20. The Lead Suspect
21. Face To Face
22. Pressure
23. An Arrest
24. The Church
25. The Defense Attorney
26. The Press
27. The Judge
28. The Trial

29. For The Defense
30. Testimony
31. Detective Musto
32. More Testimony
33. Cosing Arguments
34. The Defense Takes Its Turn
35. Jury Deliberations
36. Has The Jury Reached a Verdict?
37. Death Row
38. Call Me "PADRE"
39. The Intervening Years
40. More About Mike
41. More About Louis
42. More About Anna Ruiz
43. DNA
44. Getting An Appeal
45. Damage Control
46. Free At Last
47. Confessing a Confession
48. The Appeal
49. Making Their Case
50. Getting a DNA Sample
51. The Sting
52. Setting The Stage
53. A Conversation
54. Dna Results
55. The Hot Seat
56. The DA's Case
57. A New Trial
58. Honor Among Thieves
59. Justice
60. Epilogue

PROLOGUE

May 12th, 1963, Brooklyn, NY

He waited until both his parents were dozing off in front of the television. He thought he could complete his mission before they awoke, or that he'd sneak back into the house without them ever realizing he had left after they were in bed. He had gone to his room after dinner as usual. His parents would think he was still there when they retired for the night.

He was careful not to make any noise as he left the house. He didn't want to explain why he was leaving. Inside, he was seething. In his fifteen years on this earth, he had never been this angry. He wanted to break dishes and toss furniture around. The damn restraining the raging waters in his mind, was ready to burst allowing his turbulent anger to consume everything in it's path.

Once out of the house, he let out a primal scream. He turned over a neighbor's trash can on his way to the bus stop. He couldn't control his anger. Lights came on as some neighbors opened their doors to see what was causing all the commotion. He ignored their comments and made his way to the corner bus stop. He had no money for the fare, but the driver saw the insane look on the young boy's face and allowed him to ride for free.

He had tried desperately to put what had happened behind him, but nothing had worked. He realized he needed retribution. He wanted revenge. He would go to the police. That would insure the person responsible for his torment would be punished, put in prison, and his life ruined.

The bus ride seemed to take forever, but he finally approached his destination. A slight grin crossed his face as he exited the bus in anticipation of what would happen next. He would finally free himself of the guilt and shame he couldn't seem to shake.

* * * *

The overworked detective was enjoying a rare moment of peace on a Saturday morning, sitting on the commode reading an old autopsy report when the phone jolted him from the paper. Quickly, he finished his business and hurried to the kitchen phone where he picked up the receiver after the tenth ring. Whoever was calling was persistent.

"Hello," he snapped. Then he heard a familiar voice. He eyed the clock on the wall which read 7:10 a.m..

"Mike, I hate to bother you at home on your day off, but there's been a murder of a young boy in the cafeteria at a Catholic school on Crown Street and Bedford Avenue. This is going to be high profile, so the captain wants you to take lead on this. The kid was butchered pretty badly with a kitchen knife. Crime Scene is on the way. Give your partner a call and have him meet you at the scene. The Medical Examiner's Office has been notified and will be there by the time you get to the scene."

"Isn't that Loyola Prep, the Jesuit High School?" Mike asked.

"Don't know for sure. You're more familiar with the area."

"On my way."

Mike disliked the interruption on a quiet Saturday morning. He had planned to catch up on errands, but was always ready when duty called. It came with the territory. He'd already put in lots of overtime without extra pay to keep up with his mounting case load. Sixty-hour weeks or more were the norm. He looked forward to the weekends to catch up with his personal needs; laundry, hair cuts, shopping for groceries and such. He was the "go to" guy in the squad who relished being called upon when things went haywire. He wondered how his newly assigned trainee would react to his first homicide. This could be a spectacular case to break in with. He thought of the irony of his new Jewish partner getting his baptism in blood working his first murder case on the grounds of a Catholic church. This would serve as a good test. After phoning Detective Maurice Gold, Mike headed to the crime scene.

Confessions, Lies, and Secrets   *Stu Milisci*

CHAPTER 1

Childhood Brooklyn, 1959

"Hey, little brother, I barely beat you this time," Louis exclaimed. I used to beat you by two houses and today I had to run my ass off just to inch you out."

Louis age 14 and Steven age 11, used to race home every evening before dinner time from the mailbox on the corner to their house half way down the block. They lived in Red Hook, a neighborhood near the Brooklyn entrance to the Battery Tunnel, connecting Brooklyn to Manhattan. The neighborhood struggled to attain middle class status. It was made up mostly of city workers such as sanitation men, bus drivers or other transit personnel. It also included many laborers. Teachers, cops, and firemen generally live in better neighborhoods.

Their father had chosen Red Hook because most residents were white. Their ancestors had come from Europe during hard times in countries such as Germany, Poland, Ireland, and Italy. He felt they would be safer and

Confessions, Lies, and Secrets   *Stu Milisci*

more secure there than poorer neighborhoods which were predominately black and Puerto Rican. Old world prejudices were stowaways on the voyage across the Atlantic with the immigrants who harbored them.

Louis was a freshman at Loyola Prep, a Jesuit High School in Brooklyn. Steven was in the fifth grade at Our Lady Of Mercy Grammar School a few blocks from where they lived. There would be hell to pay from their father if they weren't on time for dinner every night. He insisted on eating together as a family at dinnertime to discuss the day's events and offer fatherly advice to his two sons.

The conversation at supper often emphasized the importance of a good education and being the very best you could be at everything you did. Their parents realized how important a decent education was in today's day and age since neither of them had the chance to go on past high school. Their father, Giuseppie, had migrated from Sicily with his parents when he was seventeen. Rosa, his wife, was born in America, a first generation American. While Giuseppie worked in construction, she worked in a sweatshop making women's blouses and dresses. Their life was a constant struggle and money was always tight. They made huge sacrifices for their children. Louis' high school required a significant tuition. They never complained about money, especially when it came to spending it on their son's schooling. They spoiled Louis, determined he would eventually attend a good college and become a success in life. Louis complied with their every wish.

Louis graduated from grammar school with the highest average in his class, then earned straight A's in high school while a star football and track athlete. The brothers had always been competitive, but since Lou was older, bigger and stronger, Steve could never win at anything.

Steve did well in school, but not as well as Louis. Schoolwork came much harder for Steven. He often found himself being compared to his brother yet, unable to match his accomplishments. Steven felt the pressure to qualify for the same high school as Louis.

Jesuit schools didn't just focus on reading, writing and arithmetic. They also considered literature, romance languages, and history to be equally important. Teachers weren't focused only on facts and figures, they wanted to strengthen student will and character. They wanted them to learn how to think.

Jesuit High Schools also prepared students for a life espoused by the priests devoted not only to personal achievement and growth, but more importantly, to the betterment of all mankind. These were the values that mattered to Giuseppi and Rosa Caruso. This is why they made so many sacrifices to send their sons to a Jesuit High School.

Eighth grade finally arrived for Steven and with it the entrance exam for the Jesuit high school. Boys from all five boroughs, including Long Island, were competing for a spot in that school.

Three years earlier, Louis had placed third on the list for acceptance.

Steve was 153rd out of 165. Nevertheless, he had made it and that was all that mattered to him. On the day of orientation, the new freshman class gathered in the school auditorium as the headmaster, Father Watson, read the

Confessions, Lies, and Secrets   *Stu Milisci*

names of the new students. When he got to Steven Caruso, he asked, "Are you Caruso's brother?"

"No, I'm Caruso. Louis is my brother." A chuckle was heard from the classmates while a stern look crossed Father Watson's face.

Steven didn't want to start off the first day of school living in his brother's shadow. He felt he was his own person and wanted to be accepted for what he was capable of doing. His first day of school began with a wise crack to the headmaster.

CHAPTER 2

The Calling April, 1952

James Savino was impaled on the horns of a dilemma. He was the only child of Italian parents who looked forward to one day having grandchildren. But James, as a teenager, had shown little interest in girls and had always wanted to become a priest. He didn't want to disappoint his parents by not giving them grandchildren, but felt they would be proud of him anyway if he entered the priesthood. He had been an altar boy in grammar school and was mesmerized by the priests performing a wedding or conducting a funeral service. He saw how the congregants respected and admired them. He saw priests as more important and powerful than policemen, firemen and even politicians. On Sundays, he sat awestruck listening to sermons delivered from the lecterns. He scanned the reactions of the faithful in attendance and realized the power of the man holding court in this, most sacred of all places. He wanted that power.

Confessions, Lies, and Secrets *Stu Milisci*

As a gangly, dark haired and handsome high school senior, James Savino fully realized his calling to the priesthood at the same high school where he later taught as part of his journey to becoming a Jesuit Priest. His interests revolved around the debating team, the drama society, and all things intellectual. After high school, he entered the seminary, earned his degree in Christian Theology, took his initial vows and became a teaching scholastic at Loyola Jesuit High School, part of the requirements for being ordained. As a member of the faculty, he joined many of the priests who taught there while he was a student. He began teaching when Louis Caruso was a sophomore.

Everyone knew Louis, a standout both academically and athletically. Louis would soon be on his way to Boston College on a full scholarship. James Savino took a special interest in Louis not only because of his extraordinary intelligence and athletic ability. They both shared the same Italian heritage. He often counseled Louis, aware of his humble circumstances and encouraged him to work hard at everything he did. Louis enjoyed the attention and often asked Savino for his advice and counsel. Savino helped Louis prepare his college entrance resume extolling his many accomplishments in high school, which probably helped a lot in his getting a scholarship to Boston College.

James Savino had been teaching for two years and had excellent ratings and evaluations when Steven became a freshman. Savino was held in high esteem by other members of the faculty. They evaluated him based on his devotion to work, willingness to help the students, and his likeable personality. Father Watson, the current headmaster, knew him from the time he was a student at the school. Students liked Savino because he was much younger than the priests, and could relate better with their problems. Besides, he had a wicked jump shot.

Louis' younger brother, Steven, along with 22 incoming freshmen was assigned to James Savino's class. Since the teacher had known Louis, he dubbed Steven the class "Beetle," an assignment which designates a teacher's helper.

On his first day of school, Steven was being singled out because of his older brother. Two faculty members who would be the most influential in his future schooling had already taken notice of him.

Confessions, Lies, and Secrets   *Stu Milisci*

CHAPTER 3

The Mean Streets Manhattan-1924/ 1941

Most people agreed Andy Watson was a tough bastard. He had to prove that every day on the mean streets of the Hell's Kitchen neighborhood on the west side of Manhattan where he was born and raised. The neighborhood was made up of Irish, Italian and black residents who were always fighting with each other or among themselves. As a teenager, Andy often fought with older and bigger boys, but he never backed down and rarely got the worst of it in the mini wars. He not only was respected, he was feared. Most of the other teen-aged boys had the good sense to steer clear of him.

Actually a bastard, Andy was born from a mother who had become pregnant at sixteen, forced to quit school to raise her son. The boy never met his father who was arrested and sent to prison for a robbery before Andy was born. His father never returned to Hell's Kitchen after being released from prison.

Confessions, Lies, and Secrets　　　　　　　　*Stu Milisci*

    Andy and his mother lived with her parents for a short time, but her Irish Catholic upbringing made it difficult for an unwed mother and her newborn son. She had disgraced her parents when having a child outside of wedlock was frowned upon by the community and the church. Eventually, she secured her own small apartment nearby when Andy was two years old. It was all she could afford, but it was clean and comfortable. She worked at The Carlyle Hotel on East 76th Street on the fashionable East Side of Manhattan cleaning rooms and doing laundry. She had a second job cleaning the homes of wealthy residents on Riverside Drive. Andy learned a great deal about sacrifice from his mother at a very early age.

    Andy's grandmother was a bitter woman who would not forgive her daughter for disgracing the family. She babysat for little Andy while his mother worked, though he spent much of his time alone, feeling unloved. He found the streets of Hell's Kitchen at a very early age.

    After grammar school, Andy was admitted to LaSalle Academy, a Catholic high school on East Second Street and Third Avenue in lower Manhattan. He got into fights almost daily on the subway train. The school was located near a men's shelter and an apartment house where The Hell's Angels motorcycle gang lived around the corner. He frequently faced off against bigger boys on his way to and from school never backing down from a fight.

    Ethnic groups in the neighborhood stuck together. They formed street gangs for neighborhood supremacy, The Blacks had the "Bloods" and the "Crypts." Their main activity and source of revenue came from drug sales. The Italians would do favors for the older wise guys in hopes of being accepted into a Mafia family when they became of age. The Irish formed gangs of their own called "The Westies." They started out committing minor crimes like larceny and purse snatching, eventually upping the ante to extortion, loan sharking, and contract murder. Being Irish, Andy joined "The Westies."

While In high school, Andy was arrested with other gang members for breaking into a warehouse on the west side docks. At the arraignment, a merciful judge let him decide between prison or the Armed Forces. Andy opted for choice "B" and enlisted in the Navy. From there he arrived at the Great Lakes for his basic training.

* * * *

Steven Caruso, James Savino, and Andy Watson seemed to have little in common growing up, but their lives were destined to intertwine.

Confessions, Lies, and Secrets   *Stu Milisci*

CHAPTER 4

World War 1942/1944

Andy enjoyed his time in basic training, having never left Manhattan in his entire life. A whole other world existed out there that he had never experienced. No longer did he have to fight every day to survive. Everything he needed was provided. On weekend passes, Andy would sit on the shoreline of Lake Michigan and revel in the fresh air and the sun shimmering off the water.

After basic training, Andy reported to his new station in Hawaii, assigned as the chaplain's assistant. The elderly Irish priest, Father Timothy Rooney, was loved and respected by everyone, like a favorite uncle.

If the Great Lakes were a revelation to Andy, then Hawaii was paradise. He never imagined such beautiful places existed anywhere on earth. Warm climate and ocean breezes prevailed. The vegetation and the food were magnificent. The natives were warm and friendly.

Confessions, Lies, and Secrets   *Stu Milisci*

      Though peaceful on base, the war raged in Europe. Everyone knew America would soon get involved. Italy had allied itself with Germany, while Japan had entered the fray in the Pacific. German Chancellor, Adolf Hitler, was pushing through Europe and committing horrible atrocities. The Prime Minister of Great Britian, Neville Chamberlain, signed The Munich Pact with Germany in 1938, which ceded parts of Czechoslovakia to Germany. A year later, Hitler violated The Munich Pact by invading Czechoslovakia and Poland. After Hitler's forces entered Poland, Chamberlain officially declared war on Germany. Winston Churchill took over as Prime Minister of England in 1940 and managed to secure war supplies, (ammunition, guns, tanks, planes, etc.,) from America, but the United States refused to enter the war.

      Andy was there on December 7, 1941, which started out as a typical beautiful day in Hawaii, but early in the morning, the sound of fighter planes could be heard coming from the west by everyone on the base. A group of Japanese warplanes attacked the base at Pearl Harbor killing 2403 and wounding 1178 people, mostly servicemen. In total The United States lost twenty one ships in the surprise attack, which served as the catalyst for the United States entering World War II.

      As the first planes attacked, Father Rooney left the barracks and headed for the pier where many ships had been struck. Andy grabbed the old priest's wrist to try to stop him from heading into danger. Although Andy had grown up a tough kid in a bad neighborhood, nothing he ever experienced on the streets of Hell's Kitchen could have prepared him for what he was now in the middle of.

He didn't feel afraid, but had no idea what he should do. He was more concerned with Father Rooney's safety than his own.

"Father, you can't go out there. You'll probably get killed."

Father Rooney pulled his hand away from Andy's grip with strength that belied the old man's age and replied, "Andrew, I must go out there and tend to the wounded and the dead. You can stay here if you want, but I must go do my job."

For the first time in his short life, Andy realized what true courage was. It wasn't the false bravado of the bullies on the street back in Hell's Kitchen. It was this frail old man risking his life in service to others. Inspired by the old priest's bravery, Andy answered, "Okay, Father. I'm with you all the way."

Father Rooney paused and took Andy's hand in his. He looked directly into his eyes. The old priest's eyes conveyed a message of strength, compassion, and determination. At that moment, Andy realized this man was the strongest, most courageous, and most honest person he had ever met. "Andrew, are you familiar with scripture?" Father Rooney asked.

"Yes, Father," Andy replied, "I have a Catholic education."

Father Rooney continued, "When Christ was being crucified, he was placed on a cross and stationed between two thieves. One of the thieves repented. One of the last things Christ said before he died is something I will repeat to you now. He said, 'This day thou shalt be with me in paradise.'"

Confessions, Lies, and Secrets   *Stu Milisci*

Father Rooney was indefatigable in the days and weeks following the attack. Andy constantly remained by his side as he consoled the families of those killed or injured while counseling the survivors. Andy was so impressed with the old priest's energy and ability to minister to people of all faiths, he decided, then and there, the priesthood was his calling.

When his enlistment was over, Andy was a changed man returning to his mother's Hell's Kitchen apartment. He worked in construction and enrolled in night school. He had no time to hang out with his old buddies, which kept him out of trouble.

After seven tough years of work and school, he obtained his degree and became accepted in a Jesuit seminary. Three years later he took his initial vows and was assigned to teach at a Brooklyn high school as a requirement to be ordained. He taught at Loyola Jesuit High School, where, years later, he would serve as Headmaster. After he fulfilled all his requirements, he was ready to be ordained.

By this time, Father Rooney was no longer able to function as a priest and he lived in a residence for elderly priests on the campus of Fordham University. Andy was pleased to see him at his ordination at St. Patrick's Cathedral in Manhattan. The ordination of priests, known as the sacrament of Holy Orders, is one of the most beautiful and ceremonious rituals of the church. It is presided over by a bishop and involves much symbolism such as candidates for priesthood lying prone on the floor beneath the altar and the laying on of hands by the bishop conveying the transfer of power from him to the candidates.

Father Rooney gave Andy a gold crucifix and chain, which his father had given him as a gift at his own ordination more that forty years prior. He had an inscription etched on the back of the crucifix, which was written in Latin. It read,"Ad Maiorem Dei Gloriam". Translated it reads, "To the greater glory of God," which is the Latin motto for the Jesuit order. Andy accepted the gift with the promise he would wear it every day as Father Rooney had in Hawaii.

Confessions, Lies, and Secrets   *Stu Milisci*

CHAPTER 5

The School

Steven's first week of school went pretty well without much fanfare. The new students were getting to know each other as well as the teachers, coaches and administrators of the school. Most students had decided what teams they would try out for and what other extra curricular activities they would engage in. The jocks were interested in football, basketball, track and baseball, while the intellectuals decided on the debating team, the school newspaper or the drama society.

    Discipline at Loyola Prep was something to be taken very seriously. One of the ways Father Watson established this was by picking up unruly students by their ears when visible to the new boys. Notes would be sent to the parents of the offending students.

    All the boys knew Father Watson had been the light heavyweight boxing champion of the armed forces while on active duty in Hawaii. He would stand by the front entrance of the school each morning in a tee shirt displaying his bulging biceps no matter the weather. Tardiness was not acceptable. When a student's hair touched the collar of his shirt, he would be sent to get a haircut in a barbershop around the corner. The boys speculated Father was getting a kick back from the barber. A punishment called "JUG" was levied on disobedient or unruly boys. Anyone sentenced to "JUG" had to walk around the perimeter of the school for hours on end after dismissal.

Steven had to leave home by 6:30 a.m. to be in class at 8:15. School lasted until 3:15 p.m. with a one hour lunch period. Most boys played football or basketball after the lunch hour. Steven's superior athletic ability was apparent to anyone watching. Mr. Savino taught Steven's first period Theology class and then Latin the last period. Since Steven was the class "Beetle", he usually stayed after class to clean the black board and tidy up. The extra time gave him a chance to talk with Mr. Savino who had taken an interest in him since he knew Steven's older brother.

Mr. Savino interrupted Steven as he was cleaning the blackboard.

"So, Steven, how'd your first week go?"

Steven put down the eraser and turned to face Mr. Savino. They were now alone in the classroom.

"So far, so good. My brother filled me in on a lot about the school and what to expect, so I really feel like I had a head start over some of the other guys in the class."

Mr. Savino told Steven to relax and take a seat as he continued the conversation.

"Have you thought about trying out for the football team? Your brother was an extraordinary football player and that helped him get a free ride to Boston College. I'm sure Coach Riley would like to see you come out for the team."

As he was speaking, Mr. Savino took a seat next to Steven.

"I'm a lot smaller than my brother, and the school doesn't have a junior varsity team, so I doubt I'd make the varsity. Maybe I'll wait a year and see if I get a little bigger.

Leaning a little closer to Steven, Mr. Savino continued. "Your brother was a running back and linebacker. You may be smaller than him now, but I've seen you playing during lunch break and you're a lot faster than he was. You'd be a great wide receiver or defensive back. I'm not the only one who noticed you. Coach Riley was watching one day and he asked me if I could convince you to come out for tryouts."

"To tell you the truth, I'd like to try out for the team. I'll give it a shot. I have nothing to lose I guess."

Mr. Savino leaned in a little closer and put his hand on Steven's shoulder in a reassuring manner.

"Don't sell yourself short young man. Have confidence and you'll do fine whether it's football or school work. You can go as far as you want as long as you're willing to do the work."

"Thanks for the vote of confidence, Mr. Savino. I think I will try out for the team."

"I think you'll be surprised at how well you'll do. Steven, you can call me Jim after class. I'm only Mr. Savino in the classroom."

Confessions, Lies, and Secrets   *Stu Milisci*

Steven was a little surprised and uncomfortable by what his teacher had told him. His older brother had never referred to any of his teachers or coaches by their first name and he had spent four years at the school and had been very popular among the faculty.

"Okay. Mis tah Jim. Anything else before I leave?"

"No, Steven. The classroom looks pretty good. See you bright and early in the morning."

Steven tried out for the football team and, to his delight, he made the varsity. He was the only freshman to make the team mostly because he had beaten everyone in the time trials for the forty yard dash including juniors and seniors who were older, bigger and stronger than he. Those races with his brother from the mailbox to the dinner table had paid off. He generally played only on the practice squad, but he traveled to the away games and played on special teams. He managed to play in a few plays as a defensive back to give a breather to players who played both offense and defense.

The team had five wins and three losses that season despite the loss of his brother, Louis, who had gone on to college. Mr. Savino encouraged Steven to try out for the track team after the football season. Steven did well at the tryouts and at the first indoor track meet, he surprised everyone by what he did in the junior varsity mile relay. Steven ran the final leg. When he got the relay baton, his team was in third place, half a lap behind the leading team. The armory track was a 160 yard oval. Each team member ran a quarter of a mile. Steven took the baton and overtook the other 2 runners. His team won the race. His 51.6 seconds time was unbelievable for a freshman who had

never run a quarter mile before. His performance at his first track meet was noticed by every one in attendance. The school paper ran the headline,
"Another Caruso Hits The Track."

Confessions, Lies, and Secrets   *Stu Milisci*

CHAPTER 6

Baiting The Hook

James Savino had gone to all the football games that season whether they were played at home or away. He also tried to make as many track meets as his schedule would allow. After each game and track meet he always made it a point to find Steven, compliment him on his performance and encourage him to do even better at his next game or track meet. He reminded Steven how important it was to have a diverse resume to submit for college entrance. He emphasized academics were important, but so were sports activities, plus social and community involvement.

One day after classes when Steven and the teacher were again alone in the classroom, James took a seat next to Steven and stated,

"So, Steven, the election for class officers is coming and I think you should run for class president. It would look great on your college entrance applications to show you were freshman class president, and maybe you can parlay that into Student Council President in your senior year."

Steven had thought about running but lacked the confidence. Mr. Savino's suggesting it to him made him reconsider.

"I'll give it a shot if you think I have a chance, Jim. But I don't know about Student Council President."

James placed a hand on Steven's shoulder as was his custom when he wanted to drive home a point or reassure Steven of something. "There you go again, selling yourself short. Your grades are good enough to earn the silver medal for freshman year for the second highest average overall. The gold medal is out of reach since Artie Johnson is a certified genius who gets 100 on every test, in every subject. He's a shoe-in for the highest overall average. Since you have me for Theology and Latin, I can help you. You've already made a name for yourself in both football and track. Everyone in the class likes and respects you."

"Okay, Jim, you haven't led me wrong so far, so I'll take your advice and run."

Steven won the election for freshman class president and continued the good grades.

Theology was taught first class in the morning for Steven's group. To make the class more interesting and try to keep the class's attention, Mr. Savino would often go on a tangent and talk about problems many boys were dealing with. One Monday morning, he started class saying, "This is a very unique time in your lives, the four years you will be spending in high school. You have come in here as boys, will be going through puberty, then adolescence, and hopefully will graduate as young men ready to go on to college and face new challenges and opportunities. While you may feel by going to a boys' only high school, you are being denied the chance of meeting young girls and interacting with them on a daily basis, you must be careful what you wish for. Not only are they a distraction, they can get you in a whole bunch of trouble. Lives are often ruined by young girls getting impregnated by classmates. The girls' lives and young men's lives are ruined. What of the unplanned infant? The girl's parents often take on the responsibility of raising the child or the boy and girl decide to get married and ruin their chances for a higher education and a bright future. While I realize teenagers go through a lot of physical changes, you must do your best to keep these changes in check."

Steven remained engrossed as Mr. Savino paced back and forth at the front of the class room, careful not to focus on any one student . His eyes roved from one to another.

"Most of you have come from Catholic grammar schools and have been brainwashed into thinking everything is a sin. This causes you to fight the forces of nature while going through these difficult years. Your physical needs require some kind of sexual release, but the church teaches even thinking about those things is a sin. I am not even ordained yet, so I'm not going to try to challenge the teachings of the church." As he continued to talk, the teacher took a seat on the front of his desk. "But, not too long ago, I was sitting where you are now sitting and going through the same trials and tribulations you're

Confessions, Lies, and Secrets   *Stu Milisci*

going through. Remember God is all merciful, and all forgiving, and absolutely everybody sins." Mr. Savino paused and stood again. He resumed pacing back and forth at the front of the classroom.

"I hear things and see certain things myself that indicate to me some of the boys in this school are relying on one another to help satisfy those natural physical needs. While there isn't a priest in the world who would tell you this is not a grievous sin, they would also tell you satisfying those same needs by yourself is also a sin. I'm not condoning any type of homosexuality here. I don't want anyone to feel too guilty about doing some things, which are only natural. Your lives will be filled with new temptations and opportunities, which you'll have to make decisions about. Remember God is all merciful or why else would He have sent His only Son to earth to die on the cross to atone for our sins."

It was obvious from their body language some of the boys were uncomfortable with the topic of conversation. The boys exchanged quick glances from one to another while others rustled in their seats.

Steven, and presumably the others, knew exactly what Mr. Savino was talking about, and, for the most part, gave him their undivided attention. They marveled he had the courage to discuss these issues in a Theology class in a Jesuit High School. He had been right. They had never been spoken to like this before. Not in a class room. Not in church. Not even in a confessional. They had been brainwashed in the past by 'Fire and Brimstone' clerics while in grammar school, made to feel guilty about every thought, word, and action they engaged in. Steven looked around at his classmates and could see they admired Mr. Savino for his understanding of what they were going through and his willingness to discuss it with them. It built confidence in him not only as a teacher but also as an advisor and someone they felt they could trust. He, in turn, saw how they all seemed to work harder to get good grades and to avoid scrapes in school. Steven realized some older priests did not have the same understanding of their needs and feelings of guilt.

"So, boys," Mr. Savino continued, "What happens in class, stays in class. We don't need the Headmaster or the older priests snooping around this classroom. I feel an obligation not only to be your teacher, but, to help you get through a difficult time in your lives which, not too long ago, I was going through myself.

Mr. Savino could see from the expressions on the faces of most of the boys he had to change the subject to a lighter topic and made a suggestion he hoped they would agree with.

"On the Saturday night of the second week of Easter break, I'm going to ask if we can have the use of the cafeteria and the gym so we can have a 'class night' at the school. We'll shoot some hoops and have some snacks. Should be a good time. Until then, everyone have a good Easter and enjoy your vacation."

Confessions, Lies, and Secrets   *Stu Milisci*

CHAPTER 7

Hooking The Fish

Easter season came as Steven's school was in recess for eleven days from Holy Thursday until the following Monday. Home for the Easter holidays, Steven's brother, Louis, had lots to share with his little brother about life on a college campus. He said he was delighted to be chosen as the starting half back on the football team since most freshman were "red shirted" their first year, meaning they didn't play in any games, but practiced with the team. But Louis finally started at halfback as a freshman and was selected the conference freshman player of the year. As in high school, he was thought of highly by students and faculty alike. He emphasized the need for Steven to work hard in high school and get involved with as many extra curricular activities as he could handle. Steven took his advice to heart and told Louis about his accomplishments thus far on the football field, on the indoor track and in the classroom.

Confessions, Lies, and Secrets *Stu Milisci*

When Louis was scheduled to return to Boston College, his parents decided to drive him up and spend the weekend in Boston. They had never been to Boston nor had a chance to see the campus. Steven said he'd be fine remaining at home, he had a class at school that night.

All 23 students in James Savino's freshman class showed up for the "Class Night" even though attendance wasn't mandatory. This demonstrated how much the boys liked and respected their teacher and counselor. After playing basketball in the gym a few hours, Mr. Savino treated the class to pizzas and cokes in the cafeteria, paid for from his own pocket. It was about 10:00 p.m. when he suggested the boys hit the showers since they had told their parents to pick them up at the school around 10:30. Steven and Mr. Savino remained alone in the cafeteria.

"Steven, if you give me a hand cleaning up the cafeteria, I'll give you a ride home after you shower."

"I'd be happy to help you straighten up, Jim, but I can take the bus home. I take it every day to and from school. It runs every twenty minutes until midnight."

Mr. Savino responded, "I wouldn't think of letting you go home by bus alone at this hour of the night. Not in this neighborhood. Maybe we can stop at the A & W on the way home and get a root beer float. I've always had a weakness for those things. It's settled. Now go shower and I'll meet you in the locker room in about fifteen minutes."

Steven finished helping Mr. Savino tidy up and headed to the showers. The locker room seemed deserted and the other boys had apparently been picked up by their parents. But when Steven got to his locker, he heard what sounded like soft whimpering coming from one of the aisles. Steven investigated and found the class genius, Artie Johnson, sitting on a bench, crying softly.

Steven felt sure something bad had happened to his classmate. "Artie, what's wrong? Did someone pick on you? Are you all right?"

"Oh, no Steven. It's that bully Joey Tedesco teasing me in front of everybody about how small I am. I was embarrassed to get into the shower with the other guys. They all have body hair and big joints and I look like a little kid next to them, especially with no clothes on."

Steven felt compassion for the boy. He had witnessed other boys picking on him before and felt obligated as class president to take a stand in defense of him. "Artie, you skipped a couple of grades in grammar school because you're so freakin' smart. You're two years younger than most of these guys. The guys who bully and tease you only do it because they're jealous. You'll get body hair and grow bigger in due time, but the others will be jerks for the rest of their lives. You outshine these other guys in so many ways. If you want, I'll talk with Tedesco and straighten him out."

"Oh, no, Steven. Thanks for offering, but I can deal with the bullying. You've made me feel a lot better though. Thanks for talking to me. If there's ever anything I can do for you, just say the word."

Steven and Artie continued talking as Artie dressed and left to catch his ride home. Steven headed for the showers.

Steven was a little surprised, but not embarrassed when Mr. Savino stuck his head inside to let him know that he was waiting for him to finish his shower so they could leave.

"Steven, it's amazing. You have the body of a mature adult at fifteen years old."

Steven chuckled and responded jokingly, "Well, Jim, you know how it is with us Italians. We're taller than our grandmothers when we're ten and start shaving when we're eleven. But we usually stop growing when we're twelve."

"Well, it's plan to see, parts of you are all grown up already."

Steven thought it was a little strange for Mr. Savino to be making these kind of comments, but shook it off.

"Okay Jim, I'll be through in a minute."

Steven finished showering, toweled himself dry, and got dressed. He and his teacher walked out to the parking lot where they got into the parish car and left for home with a detour at the A&W Root Beer stand. There were times Steven thought of Mr. Savino more as an older brother than a teacher. He really enjoyed his alone time with Jim and the conversations they had.

After finishing their floats and hot dogs, Mr. Savino drove a few blocks then pulled to the curb on a deserted, dimly lit street and parked.

Steven felt confused and asked, "Jim, is something wrong? Are you all right? Why are we stopping?"

"No, I'm fine. I wanted to talk with you before I take you home." As he was talking, Mr. Savino turned toward Steven, laid his right hand on the upper thigh of Steven's left leg and began rubbing it.

Steven was startled by this. His heart began to race. He fumbled for the door release but couldn't find it. He wanted to get out of that car as fast as he could.

"Jim, I don't know what's going on here, but I don't think I like it very much."

Savino smiled, "Steven, I can tell you like it because I can feel what's happening inside your pants."

"I can't help it. That's a normal physical reaction. But my head is telling me I don't like where this is going. This feels wrong to me. I'd like you to stop it right now."

Savino continued his assault saying, "Steven, everybody does things that are wrong. The Pope in Rome, the saints in heaven have all done things that are wrong. It's human nature to sin, and we all sin because we're all human. Relax and enjoy it."

Meanwhile, Savino was unbuttoning Steven's pants and pulling down his fly with his right hand. He now had a firm grip on Steven's erect penis, and he leaned over and began sucking on it.

Steven began to cry and pleadingly asked Savino to stop, but In spite of all his protests, Steven had an involuntary orgasm in about five seconds. Mr. Savino helped clean up the mess with napkins he had taken from the A&W stand.

Savino rubbed Steven's shoulder, "Steven, I can tell. You really enjoyed that. It sure beats jerking off and I know every boy your age jerks off a lot. What difference does it make how you satisfy your sexual and physical desires as long as you're not hurting anyone else? This will always remain our little secret as long as you don't tell anyone about it. I certainly won't."

Steven pulled away from James' grasp and responded with a trebling voice, "I'm really confused about this. I had no clue what you intended to do when you pulled the car over. I didn't enjoy it at all and wish it hadn't happened. Normally I wouldn't hesitate to talk to you about something like this if it had happened with someone else. But how can I talk to you about it when you are the someone else. Please, take me home."

Savino was surprised by Steven's reaction. He tried to reassure his student. "Steven, you should know by now there isn't anything you can't talk to me about. Have I ever given you bad advice? Haven't I always looked out for your interests?"

"Sure, sure you have. But this is different."

"No—no it isn't. This is another part of the special relationship we have developed with one another. Let me take you home now and please, PLEASE, don't worry about what happened. It isn't really a big deal."

But it was a big deal to Steven, a very big deal. When he got home he was glad his parents were in Boston and wouldn't be home until the following night. He knew he needed time to compose himself and get things straight in his mind. If his parents were home, they'd probably sense something was seriously wrong and probe him about what was troubling him. He might have been able to talk about what had happened with his brother, but only in person, and that wasn't possible now since Louis had gone back up to school. For the time being, he had to keep it to himself and learn how to cope with it some way. The flashbacks haunted him. How could he have let that happen? Why hadn't he put up a struggle? He surely could have overpowered Savino, who wasn't a big man, or at least pushed him away and gotten out of the car. But it had been so unexpected and so sudden, he didn't have time to think of a way out. He resolved it would never happen again. He wondered, perhaps, if this was a sign he was gay. His first sexual experience had now been with a man and not some pretty co-ed he met in college. He quickly put that notion aside realizing what had happened had nothing to do with what he had wanted.

    During the first of many sleepless nights, Steven continued to second guess what he could have, or should have done. He wondered if it was him who had done something wrong, not realizing he was not at all to blame. He lay awake constantly burdened by overwhelming feelings of guilt.

    Two days later, Steven and his classmates returned to school. Mr. Savino seemed no different than before Easter vacation. Both periods were consumed with discussions about the class night the boys had enjoyed two days prior. At the end of the last period, Steven stayed behind to get the classroom cleaned up as he did most days. He excused himself early saying he had to go to track practice.

    Savino had been perched on the front of his desk watching Steven tidy up. "Steven, have you given any thought about what happened the other night?"

    "Are you kidding? Given any thought? It's all I've been able to think about. I can't get it out of my head as much as I want to."

Confessions, Lies, and Secrets　　　　　　　　　　*Stu Milisci*

Savino raised his hands over his head, spread them wide and raised his head for emphasis "I hope you realize the sun still rose this morning and the stars are still in alignment in spite of what we did the other night."

Steven turned and faced his teacher, "What *we* did? Don't you mean what *you* did?"

"You were there too, and you seemed to be a willing participant."

Mr. Savino had taken a seat and tried to make a tense situation less stressful.

"I had no idea what was going on in that car until it was too late. I haven't had a decent night's sleep since you attacked me in the car. If you ever try that with me again, I'll kick the shit out of you."

Mr. Savino leaped out of his chair and walked menacingly toward Steven.

"Hold on there young man. Do you think that's the proper way to talk to a teacher?"

Steven walked toward Savino with fire in his eyes. "A *teacher*? You call yourself a teacher? You've lost any credibility you may have had with me as a teacher. I'll stay in this school and put up with you for the rest of the semester, but keep far away from me or else you're going to be in a whole lot of trouble."

Savino stopped in his tracks and spoke in a softer tone "I'm sorry you feel that way. But you will give me the respect I deserve as a teacher or else you'll be the one in a whole lot of trouble."

Steven had a difficult time restraining himself. How could this pedophile expect to be respected after what he had done?

"I'll treat you the same as all the other teachers. Just stay away from me."

Steven tried his best to continue his classes, though his grades began to tumble. He started to lose interest in track, which was noticeable during practice and at the track meets. His coaches asked him what was wrong, but he didn't tell anyone what was troubling him. He couldn't shake the guilt he felt over what had happened. He felt he needed to tell someone to help lift the burden he carried. He certainly couldn't tell his parents, his brother was away at school, and Mr. Savino was the only faculty member he ever felt comfortable enough with to share personal matters.

Confessions, Lies, and Secrets   *Stu Milisci*

CHAPTER 8

Guilt And Forgiveness

"Bless me, Father, for I have sinned."
　　Steven decided to rely on his faith and teaching as a Catholic to try and rid his conscience of the guilt he felt. He remembered how good he always felt after confessing his sins and leaving the confessional with a clear head. He waited until the confessional of Father Watson was available since Steven trusted him the most of all the priests at the school.
　　"It has been three weeks since my last confession."
　　"And what are your sins, my son?"
　　Steven paused as the words got stuck in his throat, "Father, I'm ashamed to confess this, but I had sex with another man."
　　Father Watson had been an ordained priest for many years and had been the Headmaster of an all boys Jesuit High School. He had heard many confessions, so these revelations were unlikely to be a shock to him.

Confessions, Lies, and Secrets *Stu Milisci*

"When you say, 'You had sex', describe more clearly the act. What type of sex?"

"It was oral sex."

"Did you perform oral sex on him or did he perform oral sex on you?"

"He performed it on me."

"When you say, 'another man,' was he a classmate?"

"No, Father, he was a teacher."

"Did you engage in this act willingly?"

"No, Father. I did not."

"Did this other man, this *teacher*, force you to submit to this act?"

"No, Father. Not exactly."

Father asked somewhat confused, "Well if you didn't do this willingly, and you weren't forced to do it, how did it happen?"

Steven had gone to confession to relieve the burden of his sin, clear his conscience and receive absolution. He didn't want to mention Mr. Savino's name or to let anyone know who had assaulted him. He was embarrassed to tell anyone, including a priest at confession, about the sordid details of what had taken place that night. So he delicately recounted what had happened in the car without going into the sordid details and without mentioning anyone's name. Father Watson would certainly know one of his faculty members, and quite possibly a priest or scholastic, had committed this immoral act. It was also apparent the young man making the confession didn't want to reveal the identity of his attacker.

Father Watson said reassuringly, "My son, you are not guilty of any sin. This man, this *teacher* whose identity you foolishly feel obligated to conceal, committed a grievous, serious sin. He used his authority over you to force you to engage in conduct against your will. From this confessional, I cannot order you to tell the authorities, whether they be at school or the police, the identity of this person. I implore you, it's very important to reveal his identity. A person capable of an act like that should be punished and has no place teaching here or anywhere else. You have an obligation to the other students in this school to protect them from this *teacher.* You came here seeking absolution and you are absolved. Say a rosary and leave here with a clear conscience."

Confessions, Lies, and Secrets *Stu Milisci*

CHAPTER 9

The Confrontation

Steven's relief from having gone to confession was short lived. His conscience continued to haunt him, He couldn't shake the cloak of guilt he felt. He knew Father Watson could not reveal anything he had told him in the confessional, but he sensed the priest may have known the identity of the perpetrator. The priest had advised Steven he should inform the police. Steven only wanted to forget about the incident and go on with his life as if it had never happened. Telling the police, or anyone else, would only serve to keep the incident fresh in his mind. But erasing it from his memory was easier said than done. He still suffered from insomnia, his marks were falling and he had lost all interest in sports, which became apparent to his coaches. He tried going through all the motions as if nothing was bothering him, but he failed miserably.

He wondered if Mr. Savino had ever done anything like this before. His brother, Louis, never said anything to make Steven think that he was a homosexual or a pedophile. He was a man who students could approach with problems. Steven also considered that his silence was jeopardizing others to be subjected to the same abuse in the future. He thought about Father Watson's words and realized he had an obligation to protect future potential victims by going to the police and identifying Savino.

Steven finally made up his mind. He hated the thought of some other boy going through the same terrible ordeal he had suffered through because of his silence. He knew he didn't owe Mr. Savino any special consideration. He shouldn't be teaching in a boys' school. He deserved to be punished for what he had done. Never the less, Steven felt obligated to let Savino know of his decision to go to the police. Perhaps he wanted to hear Savino plead with him not to turn him in. Perhaps he wanted to hear the panic and fear in his voice.

Steven called Savino Friday night and told him what he was going to do the next morning. Savino pleaded with him not to go saying nothing good would come from it. He was surprised and shocked Steven would react this way. Going to the police would only hurt the both of them. His plans to become a priest would be railroaded, and Steven would carry a stigma with him for the rest of his life. He also told Steven, in the absence of any evidence to verify his story, he would deny these allegations and it would be Steven's word against his. The police were more likely to believe an adult on his way to becoming a priest than a teenager who might have felt slighted by something a teacher might have said or done to rub him the wrong way.

Savino pleadingly made a suggestion, "Steven, come to the cafeteria tonight so we can talk about this before you make a terrible mistake. I'll leave the side door unlocked so you can get in. No one will know you were here or be able to see you coming or leaving. Wait until ten o'clock. By then all the faculty members will be at the rectory."

* * * *

For some reason he couldn't explain or understand, Steven agreed to meet Mr. Savino in the cafeteria. He knew it was a bad idea to allow Savino to try to talk him out of going to the police once he had made up his mind. Maybe he wanted to see his face when he told him he was going to give him up and end his hopes of becoming a priest. Maybe he wanted revenge.

His parents were dozing off in front of the television unaware Steven left the house so late at night. That was good because he didn't want to have to explain where he was going. He took the bus to the school and arrived after ten o'clock. He found the door to the cafeteria unlocked and entered.

Meanwhile, James Savino was planning his strategy. He hoped he'd convince Steven not to go to the police, but he needed an alternate plan if he couldn't talk him out of it. Otherwise, his dreams of becoming a priest would be over. He also knew he would probably go to jail. He would have no alternative but to kill Steven if he couldn't convince him to remain silent.

Confessions, Lies, and Secrets　　　　　　　　*Stu Milisci*

  He would stab him to death in the cafeteria and leave his body there where it wouldn't be discovered until sometime the next morning. All the scholastics and priests who lived in the rectory had access to the school cafeteria as well as lay workers in the cafeteria and the janitorial staff. The police would suspect any one of a number of people who had access to the school. Or, perhaps, one of the other students might have been able to obtain a key. He must assure no suspicion would fall on him.

  Savino took a position in the cafeteria next to a drawer containing an array of cutlery. He chose the biggest and sharpest of the knives, which he would use to stab Steven to death if he couldn't talk him out of going to the police.

  He struggled to think of how to point suspicion on someone else to steer the police away from him as a suspect. Then, a brainstorm! He remembered how Father Watson always wore a gold crucifix around his neck. He thought it unlikely he slept with it. Thus, after killing Steven, he would enter Father Watson's room, remove the gold crucifix, and place it at the crime scene incriminating Father Watson in Steven's murder. Satisfied his plan would work, he awaited Steven's arrival.

  Savino worked himself into a frenzy by the time Steven got to the school. So confident his plan of framing the Headmaster would work, he decided to scrap his plan to talk Steven out of going to the police. He would kill him as soon as he entered the cafeteria.

  The moment Steve entered the cafeteria, Savino immediately attacked him with one of the butcher knives. Seeing this coming, Steven was able to ward off the first blow with his forearm, causing a deep wound to his right arm rendering it useless to him. Steven picked up a metal folding chair with his left hand and tried to strike Savino in the head. Savino deflected the chair with his free arm and shoulder, but one of the chair legs struck him on the side of the head. The battle continued as Steven made a desperate attempt to save his life. But he was no match for a man armed with a butcher knife and one of his own arms incapacitated. Chairs in the cafeteria were turned over and tables were displaced during the struggle.

After stabbing Steven several more times and convinced he would bleed out, Savino went ahead to phase two of his plan. He went to the rectory. By this time, all the scholastics and priests who lived there had retired to their own rooms for the night and most were either asleep or catching up with correspondence. The hallways were dark and the only light came from under the door sills of the bedrooms. Savino went to Father Watson's room and stood outside in the hallway. He could hear the sound of snoring. As he peeked in from the hallway, he saw a motionless lump in the bed. Satisfied Father Watson was fast asleep, Savino entered the room and proceeded to the night table where he saw three objects illuminated by a night light; a pair of eye glasses, a wristwatch and, BINGO, a gold crucifix on a gold chain. Savino took the crucifix and chain from the night table.

Upon returning to the cafeteria, everything was exactly as when he had left except for Steven, who now appeared to be dead. He was lying, face down, on the cafeteria floor in the middle of a large pool of blood. Savino placed the crucifix and chain in Steven's right hand

and placed that hand under Steven's body. He felt sure when the police investigated and found the crucifix it would lead directly to Father Watson. No suspicion would fall on him. Savino then turned up the overturned chairs, moved the tables back to where they had been, and checked the scene for anything which might point to him as the assailant.

Convinced his cover up plan would work, Savino returned to his room. He hadn't noticed any light coming from under the door of any rooms in the rectory, so he felt sure everyone was asleep. He undressed, took a hot shower, donned fresh pajamas, and brought the clothes he had been wearing to the furnace. He returned to his room and went to bed.

* * * *

Sean Shay had been a parishioner of Loyola Parish back when Father Watson was a scholastic teaching at the high school. He had been a hopeless drunk. His wife had left him and taken their three children with her. He had lost his job, his family and his good name somewhere at the bottom of a bottle of gin. The pastor at the time offered him a job as custodian and janitor of the rectory and school. Mr. Shay was grateful for the job and hadn't had a drink since. Saturday morning, Mr. Shay entered the school at about 6:30 a.m.. He went to the cafeteria to light the ovens and start a pot of coffee, the first chores every day. When he entered the cafeteria, he saw the body of a young boy lying on the floor, in a pool of blood. It was obvious, whoever it was had bled to death. Mr. Shay was horrified. If any alcohol were available, he would have ended his sobriety. The first person he had to notify was Father Watson, so he went to the rectory and found the priest was still asleep. He awakened him and told him what he had discovered. As Father Watson dressed, he couldn't find his crucifix where he usually left it on the night table. But, in light of what he had been told, he didn't worry about it thinking he might have misplaced it or it had fallen off the table in his hurry to get dressed.

When Father Watson entered the cafeteria with Mr. Shay, the body lying on the floor was lifeless. Shay noticed that Father Watson recognized that it was the body of one of his students, Steven Caruso. Shay stood back as Father Watson carefully avoided the crime scene. The priest then prayed and gave Last Rights. He avoided anointing the body with oil so everything would be exactly as it had been when the crime was committed. He then called the police to report the crime.

* * * *

Father Watson remembered it had been Steven who confessed about being sexually assaulted by a member of the faculty. He felt certain this murder was in retaliation for a confrontation Steven had with his attacker. He also knew, as a priest, he was obligated not to divulge anything, which had been told to him in the confessional.

The police dispatcher sent a car from the 71st precinct to investigate the report. He also dispatched an ambulance from King's County Hospital. Realizing a homicide had been committed, the uniformed officers secured the scene and placed yellow crime scene tape around the perimeter of the cafeteria. When the ambulance arrived, officers told the paramedic not to enter the taped off area. It was obvious there was no life in the body on the floor. All the cops needed from the paramedic was a name of who made the death determination for their report. They didn't want anyone to unnecessarily disturb the crime scene. The officers then called dispatch to request a Medical Examiner, a crime scene unit, and a detective team, as is customary in homicide cases.

CHAPTER 10

The Detective

Mike Musto had been a cop about as long as Father Watson had been a priest. He had also served his country during the Second World War having left high school to join the army before he graduated. Shortly after his return to civilian life, he became a New York City Police Officer. As a rookie cop in a tough Brooklyn precinct, he made a lot of quality arrests and proved to everyone he had the instincts to be a great detective. Like most good cops, he could tell from conditions, i.e. the time of day, location and actions of suspicious looking persons who seemed "Dirty", when a crime was being committed. Shortly after being assigned to a precinct as a rookie, he made a headline grabbing arrest. His precinct had been plagued by a number of robberies of elderly people on the third of each month, which was when they received their Social Security checks. Social Security recipients would receive their checks in the mail and usually go to their local bank to deposit or cash them. They became easy prey for young thugs who would rob them on their way home from the bank.

Musto was assigned to the second platoon for a day tour. The Sergeant told the officers to be vigilant to banks in their assigned area since it was check day and they were expecting the possibility of robberies of elderly people. He handed out a composite sketch which a department artist had drawn of a suspect who had been described to him by several victims.

Musto had been assigned to a foot post, which had a bank. He had reviewed past crime reports and noticed several people had been robbed after cashing their checks at that bank.

"Sergeant, do you think I can work my post in civilian clothes?" Musto asked. "There's a bank on the post and I can keep an eye on it from nearby without being noticed if I'm in civilian clothes."

The Sergeant gave Musto a look of complete disbelief.

"Musto, you're here what about two weeks out of the academy and you're asking for favors?"

Musto felt determined, "Sergeant, I feel since this bank has been hit so many times before, there's a good chance a robbery might take place there today. I'd be less conspicuous in civilian clothes. The perp in the composite probably waits somewhere nearby and when he sees a likely victim, he strikes."

"How do I know you're not looking to get lost and take off somewhere?" asked the sergeant.

"Sarge, I'll make a deal with you. Let me work in civilian clothes and if I don't make a collar, you can give me every shitty assignment that comes down the pike."

"Musto, you're new here. I was gonna do that anyway. Tell you what. I'll let you work in civilian clothes and if you *do* make a collar, I *won't* give you every shitty assignment that comes down the pike."

The sergeant knew from years of experience some of the veteran older cops wouldn't go out of their way to make a collar for a purse snatch, and often younger more eager cops would relish making collars early in their careers in hope of becoming a detective. He reluctantly allowed Musto to change into civilian clothes in hope he would make an arrest.

Musto changed into civilian clothes, took another quick look at the past crime reports and went into a coffee shop across the street from the bank, giving him an excellent view of the entire street. After his second cup of coffee, he noticed a young Black male who looked much like the person in the composite sketch, loitering in front of a bodega about two stores down from the bank's entrance. After a while, Musto saw an elderly woman walking towards the bank. She entered the bank and the suspect moved down closer to the bank in the direction the elderly woman would have to pass after leaving the bank.

Mike left the coffee shop and took up a position a few yards away from where the suspect was now standing. He figured the perp would take off in a direction opposite where the victim was likely to go once he had snatched her pocket book. Sure enough, the elderly woman left the bank and started walking toward the suspect. The suspect wrestled the pocketbook away from the old woman as soon as she was in front of him and tried to take off. Mike was on him before he could get ten steps away. Mike cuffed him

Confessions, Lies, and Secrets   *Stu Milisci*

and marched him into the station house. The sergeant and everyone else working that day were very impressed with this outstanding piece of police work.

    The following month, also on the third of the month, Mike was once again assigned to do a day tour. Again, elderly people would be heading to the bank to cash their Social Security checks. The same sergeant who gave Mike permission to work in civilian clothes the month before was turning out the second platoon. After he called the role and gave everyone their assignments, he called Musto over to the side and told him to change into civilian clothes and take the same post he had when he caught the purse snatcher the month before.

    It had made the sergeant look like a genius the previous month by putting someone on a post in civilian clothes across from a bank resulting in an arrest. Mike changed into civies and went to the same coffee shop he had gone to previously. Sure enough, after a while, the same suspect appeared in front of the same bodega he had appeared in front of the month before. He had posted bail and was back out on the streets plying his trade. This guy was no Dillinger. He was just a victim of habit.

    Mike didn't wait for any victims to appear this time. He knew one would come along eventually and the perp was sure to strike. As Mike was positioning himself, he noticed a car with three men in it park in front of the bank. The driver remained in the car and kept the motor running. The other two men left the car and entered the bank. One of them was carrying a gym bag. Mike thought it was very suspicious one of them would carry a gym bag into the bank when he could have easily left it in the car. Mike snuck up on the driver, stuck his gun into the guy's temple and handcuffed him to the steering wheel after removing the key from the ignition.

    He was sure there was a bank robbery in progress. This was before cops carried radios with them and Mike had no way of communicating what was happening to get back up from other units. He thought entering the bank in the middle of a robbery in civilian clothes brandishing a gun might lead to civilian casualties, so he decided to wait until the two other men left the bank. From his vantage point, he could see both suspicious men were armed and, indeed, a robbery was taking place. When the two suspects left the bank, Mike announced himself to be a police officer and ordered them to drop their weapons. They both fired at Mike missing him. He opened fire on them, killing one and seriously injuring the other. During the inevitable investigation and Grand Jury hearing that followed, Mike gave all the right answers and was awarded the Combat Cross, which is one of the highest awards presented in the police department.

    He continued to be a very active cop and compiled an impressive arrest record. He was promoted to third grade detective with three years on the job (a feat which no one had ever accomplished in that period of time). His observation skills were second to none. In an era when crimes were solved by a cop witnessing a crime, an eyewitness to a crime coming forward, a preponderance of evidence pointing to a suspect, or (most often) a confession, the interrogation skills of a detective were what separated the men from the boys. Mike Musto was the man.

Confessions, Lies, and Secrets   *Stu Milisci*

He would often spend many hours interrogating a suspect and asking him questions that had nothing to do with the crime being investigated. After wearing the suspect down, he would point out inconsistencies in answers the suspect had given, call him a liar, and tell him he didn't believe a word he had said. This also was before Miranda, which gave a suspect a right to remain silent, a right to an attorney during questioning, etc., etc., etc. He was able to get a lot of bad guys to make confessions with his interrogation methods. If a suspect gave him a hard time when Mike was fingerprinting him, you could sometimes hear the sound of small bones breaking in a suspect's hand while Mike rolled his fingers on the finger print paper.

He was promoted twice and was now a first grade detective, which was the highest rank a cop could obtain without passing a promotion test. Because of his skills, experience, seniority, and investigative prowess, he was often assigned the most sensitive and difficult cases coming into his precinct. He had the highest conviction rate for murder cases of anyone in the entire Police Department. Naturally, he was assigned to be the lead detective in a case involving a young boy murdered in a Jesuit institution.

Mike was happy being a detective, but a lot of bosses in the department, including the Chief of the Detectives and the Police Commissioner, encouraged him to take the sergeant's test. Usually, if a detective were promoted to sergeant, he would be transferred to another unit since it would be difficult for him to supervise the men he had worked with before being promoted. Mike didn't want to go back into uniform after being an elite first grade detective. Besides, as a first grader, he was making the same salary as a lieutenant, which was higher than top pay for a sergeant. He'd be giving up money to go back into uniform as a sergeant. He was assured by those same bosses who had encouraged him to take the promotion test, if he were promoted to sergeant, he could stay in his current squad and receive a supplementary bonus as a supervisor of detectives which would increase his salary to match that of a lieutenant's which was the same as he was making as a first grade detective.

They also told him it would be the first step in climbing the ladder to bigger and better things. Not only would it help his police career, but it would also make him a lot more desirable to the civilian market, should he leave the police department. He had no intentions of leaving the job he loved, but everyone was just one mistake away from getting fired. He had seen it happen many times. Mike took their advice. He passed the test and was assigned as a sergeant supervisor of the same detectives he had worked with for the same money he had been making as a first grade detective.

* * * *

Although Mike wasn't on duty at the time the body was discovered, he was dispatched from home to report to the scene of the murder. Upon arriving, he was happy to see the first responding uniform patrol officers had done a good job preserving the crime scene. They had cordoned off the cafeteria with yellow crime scene tape. The crime scene unit was present. They were taking photos, gathering evidence and dusting for fingerprints. A priest and a civilian custodian were also on the scene. An ambulance had come and gone after a paramedic had pronounced the victim dead.

It appeared to Mike the scene was exactly as it had been when the crime had been committed. Mike took some pictures with a Polaroid camera and carefully approached the victim. He usually didn't conduct any interviews until after he had observed the scene and reached some conclusions about how the crime had been committed. He could see the victim had been stabbed multiple times. He also noticed a defensive wound on the victim's right forearm. An overturned metal folding chair was in close proximity to the body and Musto surmised the victim had probably used this to strike his attacker. He also noticed what appeared to be some skin tissue and a clump of hair on the end of a chair leg suggesting the victim may have struck the attacker in the head and taken a chunk of scalp from him.

One of the crime scene technicians showed Mike some of the evidence that had been gathered before Mike's arrival. There was a gold crucifix on a gold chain which had a broken link which had been found in the victim's right hand. There was a butcher knife with blood on it, which was found on the floor in close proximity to the victim. These two items, along with the folding chair, would be taken to the crime lab where, after analysis for blood type, fingerprints or fiber residue, they would be secured as evidence. Mike was given photographs of all the items gathered by the crime scene unit, which would be valuable for use in his investigation.

The crucifix was of special interest to Musto. Since it had been discovered in the victim's hand, it was likely the victim had snatched it from the attacker's neck during the attack. It would be very important to the investigation to find the owner of this important piece of evidence. Upon examining the crucifix, it was evident there was an inscription on the back. Musto wasn't able to read what was inscribed because of the presence of caked up, dried blood. He instructed the crime lab technician to notify him of what the inscription read once they got the evidence back to the lab and had completed their testing.

Satisfied they had finished their work at the scene, the crime scene unit packed up their gear and left. Musto had learned the priest at the scene was the Parish Pastor and Headmaster of the school, Andy Watson. Watson informed Detective Musto there were thirty-two priests and seminarians living at the rectory. Musto realized they would all need to be interrogated and statements taken from each of them. He called his newly assigned partner, Detective Maurice Gold, at home and directed him to report to the school cafeteria.

Confessions, Lies, and Secrets *Stu Milisci*

CHAPTER 11

The Rookie

Maurice Gold was the proverbial fish out of water. He was raised in a Jewish household, had celebrated his Bar Mitzvah at age thirteen, and was, for all intents and purposes, Jewish. His family celebrated most of the Jewish Holidays, but they didn't attend Shabbat services, nor did they force their son to continue his Jewish education after his Bar Mitzvah. Maurice graduated from the prestigious Bronx High School of Science, where his interests were geared more toward journalism than science or engineering. He was an avid reader and enjoyed crime novels above all other books. After high school, he earned a Bachelor degree in psychology from New York University and then a Masters Degree in criminology from John Jay College. Many of his instructors at John Jay were high ranking members of the New York City Police Department. While cops were not allowed to moonlight working a second job, the department allowed these bosses to teach at the college.

Confessions, Lies, and Secrets *Stu Milisci*

One of his teachers, also a Jew, was an inspector in the police department. He would later rise in rank and become the cigar chomping, no nonsense Chief of Detectives. Maurice was so fascinated by what he was studying at the school, he decided to join the police department.

Because there were so few Jews in the NYPD, he had a tough time being accepted. After graduating from the academy and assigned to a precinct, he spent very little time on patrol duty. He rarely left the station house. He either worked the precinct switchboard or performed clerical duties.

He was assigned to the 60th Precinct in Coney Island. The Station House was a gothic three story building built after the civil war. Upon entering the double door entrance, you would find yourself in the turnout room with the switchboard and main desk to the right and the captain's office to the left. A three foot high brass railing stood in front of the five foot high solid mahogany desk where the tour commander held court. The switchboard was next to the main desk and Maurice spent most of his tours here or in the clerical office past the turnout room.

Most tour commanders were salty old lieutenants who wouldn't allow anyone behind the desk, but, since Maurice usually worked the switch board which you could only get to by going behind the desk, he had access to the sanctuary of the tour commander. One of the reasons the lieutenants didn't allow anyone access to the area behind the desk was because many of them would secrete a six pack of beer or a coke bottle filled with whiskey back there to help them make it through their tour of duty.

When he wasn't working the switchboard, Maurice would be working in the clerical office typing up crime reports or other police documents, which were necessary to keep things running efficiently. It was a shame he didn't get the chance to work outside on patrol too often since Coney Island was a great place for a cop to work in the summer. From Memorial Day to Labor Day, Coney Island was a huge playground. Weekends would often find close to a million people visiting to enjoy the beach, the amusements or a hot dog at Nathan's Famous.

But typing up crime reports and other documents was an education in itself. A careful study of what type of crimes were being committed in what areas and during what particular times of the day could lead a dedicated and resourceful typist to be able to make predictions based on this information and suggest how best to deploy assets to prevent future crimes. Maurice often did this and was noticed for and complimented on his work.

By now his old instructor at John Jay had risen to the rank of Chief of Detectives and, after a few years of fielding telephone calls, and typing up reports, Maurice was promoted to detective, 3d grade. It's not always what you know, but who you know that leads to advancement. Nepotism has always been alive and well in the Police Department.

His former instructor at John Jay remembered Maurice, and it also helped that they saw each other occasionally at meetings of the Shomrim Society, which was a fraternal and charitable institution within the police department made up of Jewish officers. The chief was aware of Maurice's work with crime fighting statistics and felt his talents would be a welcome addition to the detective division.

Most ethic groups within the department had their own fraternal organizations and they tended to look out for their brother members as best they could when it came to assignments or promotions. Many high ranking bosses had spent little time doing actual police work in patrol assignments. Ambitious men would somehow be assigned to administrative duties where they spent much of their time studying for promotion tests and law degrees. Once they reached the higher echelons within the department, they spent most of their time fighting perceived corruption, creating new and restrictive rules and procedures, and, in general, making the average cop's job a lot more difficult.

* * * *

Maurice was sent to the 71st precinct detective squad where Detective Sergeant Musto was assigned to be his partner. Musto had been assigned to train new detectives before, since the bosses felt his experience and expertise would help the new men acclimate to their new assignment. Musto nicknamed the new detective, Moe, because he couldn't get used to calling him Maurice. The name stuck and all the other detectives took to calling him Moe (as well as some other names which had a lot to do with his being Jewish). They often kidded him and asked how his two best friends, Larry and Curly, were doing. Moe took it all in stride and did his best to try to get along with the other detectives. They knew he had very little street experience and had been promoted to detective because he was a friend of the chief's. They joked he couldn't find a tree in the forest.

Confessions, Lies, and Secrets   *Stu Milisci*

CHAPTER 12

The Crime Scene

Mike Musto called his partner, Maurice Gold, at home and told him he had caught a fresh homicide. He gave him the location and told him to get there, ASAP.

"Okay, Mike, I'll be there in half an hour," Gold responded.

"Make that fifteen minutes. The body'll be gone in half an hour."

Detective Gold wasted valuable time gathering useless things he thought he would need for the investigation and showed up in thirty minutes and apologized for being late. It was his first homicide and he took a magnifying glass, shoe coverings, tweezers and some other items he thought would be helpful but were, in actuality, totally unnecessary. But the body was still at the scene. Mike filled him in on what he had so far.

Confessions, Lies, and Secrets   *Stu Milisci*

Moe, I want you to come with me to the rectory. We have to interview everyone who was there last night. We need to find out what each of them did from the time they finished dinner to the time they retired for the night. We also need to get written statements so we have something to compare their future statements with if we decide we need to re-interview anyone. That way we'll be able to see if there are any inconsistencies between what they tell us today and what they may tell us at some future date. Stick close to me and take notes. I'll do all the questioning."

The two detectives went to the rectory and conducted their interviews and secured the written statements of all the residents. They were able to learn only three of the faculty had Steven Caruso in any of their classes and Mr. Savino was Steven's home room teacher and guidance counselor as well as being his teacher for Latin and Theology. Other than that, not much information seemed helpful to their investigation. No one remembered seeing or hearing anything unusual or suspicious the previous night.

After finishing up at the rectory, Musto told his partner," Moe, I'm going back to the office to make some notifications and get started on the paper work. Stay here and see if you can dig up a copy of last year's school yearbook. Call the precinct where the victim lived and have a uniform unit make the notification to his parents. Have them tell the family the assigned detectives will come by later today to interview them. Stop by the Medical Examiner's office on the way back to our office and see if you can get a handle on the time and cause of death. After you've done all that, if you still want to be a detective, meet me at the office."

Gold responded, tongue in cheek, "Piece of cake, Mike. See you in about a week."

Musto headed back to the office and Gold started to tick off his assignments.

Confessions, Lies, and Secrets   *Stu Milisci*

CHAPTER 13

Suspicion

Detective Musto went to his office and began preparing the mountain of paperwork, which is generated during a homicide investigation. Notifications had to be made to the District Attorney's Office, The Chief of Detectives' Office, the NYPD Office of Public Relations for release to the news media, and a myriad of other authorities. He was still pecking away at his typewriter when his partner came in.

Disheveled and worn out, Maurice Gold reported to his superior a summary of what he had done.

"Mike, I think I did everything you asked me to. The kid lived in the 76th Precinct and his parents have been notified by the patrol unit that responded to the original call. I spoke to the cop who told them and he said they were pretty upset. They didn't even know their son had left the house and thought he was still in his room when the unit got there to make the notification. I have a school yearbook from last year. The ME was doing the Post when I got to

Confessions, Lies, and Secrets   *Stu Milisci*

his office. Cause of death was multiple stab wounds. He was up to 16 and still counting. Bled out. Figures sometime between 10:00 p.m. and midnight. I think that's everything and I still want to be a detective."

"You did great, Moe, but where's my pastrami sandwich?"

"You're kidding me, right? You didn't ask me for a pastrami sandwich. But I'll go out and get you one if you want."

"You've got promise, kid. We've both been working this case for hours and can both use a break. I'll treat you to that pastrami sandwich. After we finish lunch, we'll go interview the kid's parents. For now look, listen and learn. I'll do the talking and you just try to look professional."

CHAPTER 14

The Investigation

"Mr. Caruso, I'm Detective Musto from the 71st precinct. This is my partner, Detective Gold. We're very sorry for your loss. We're investigating the murder of your son."

"Please come in detectives," Caruso responded with a firm voice which belied his torment.

Giuseppie Caruso was a proud man hesitant to show any visible signs of emotion. He stood erect while his eyes were clear and not watery. He led the two detectives into the family living room where they saw Rosa Caruso slumped on a sofa, whimpering, looking like the air had been sucked out of her body.

"These detectives are here to ask some questions. Go into the kitchen, make some fresh coffee."

"Oh, we're fine Mr. Caruso. We don't need anything," interjected Musto.

"I prefer not to have my wife present while we speak. She is having a difficult time dealing with the loss of our son. Woman are weak and don't handle these type of things well."

Musto would have preferred to ask questions of both parents, but he respected Mr. Caruso's wishes. "That'll be fine. She doesn't need to be present. We really don't need anything except the answers to a few questions."

Rosa left the room as she had been told. Like an old fashioned Italian wife, Rosa probably did everything Giuseppie told her to do without any hesitation.

"When was the last time you saw your son?," Musto inquired.

"My wife and I were watching television and Steven went into his room after dinner at about eight o'clock. We must have both dozed off. We awoke and went to bed at about eleven o'clock. We thought Steven was either in his room or had gone out while we were dozing."

"So you didn't see him after eight o'clock and didn't know he had gone out some time after that?"

"No. Like I said, we were asleep and didn't know if he was in his room or if he had gone out."

"You wouldn't know if someone picked him up at home?"

"No. That's unlikely since none of his friends drive."

"How long would it have taken him to get to school from the house by public transportation?"

"He takes the bus on Union Street, a couple of blocks away. It usually takes him about half an hour."

Musto continued, " We think he got to the school a little before ten o'clock. So he would have had to have left the house sometime after nine o'clock."

"Like I said, we were both asleep in front of the televison, so we didn't see him leave."

"When did you realize he hadn't been home all night?"

"Not until the two officers came to our house to tell us what had happened. It was about 9:30 this morning."

Detective Musto reached into his jacket pocket and pulled out a photograph depicting a gold crucifix and chain, which he had been given at the crime scene and asked Mr. Caruso if his son had a crucifix like that.

"No," Mr. Caruso replied. "But that looks like the crucifix Father Watson wears. I've seen him with it on many occasions. Is that a clue? Is it important to the investigation?"

"It's a piece of evidence. I really can't discuss with you its value to the investigation. Do you know Father Watson well?"

"Our older boy, Louis, went to the school, so we've known Father Watson for almost five years. "

"And what do you think of him?" Musto asked.

As soon as Detective Musto showed the photo of the crucifix to Mr. Caruso, you could see a visible change in his appearance. He tried to control his emotions and answer the detective without casting any aspersions on Father Watson.

"He's very dedicated to the boys and does a fine job as headmaster. He can be a little rough with them sometimes, but sometimes you have to be. Our sons liked and respected him. He's not a suspect, is he?"

Musto continued, "Right now we have a lot of suspects. Everyone who was sleeping in the rectory last night is a suspect. We're trying to narrow the list down and your cooperation has been very helpful. Did your son have any enemies at school that you know of?

"Detective, my son was a respected athlete and president of the freshman class. He never spoke of any problems at school and had no enemies there or any where else that I know of."

Musto replied, "The officer who came to your house this morning will be in touch with you so one of you or another family member can go to the morgue and make a positive identification of Steven. Then the body will be released to you for funeral arrangements. I will keep you up to date on the progress of the investigation. We will find out who did this to your son and get justice for him."

They said their good byes and the two detectives left.

CHAPTER 15

The Evidence

On the ride back to the precinct, Moe was quiet and seemed to be a little upset.

"What's the matter, Moe? You seem pissed off."

"When were you gonna tell me about the crucifix?"

"Moe, you're my partner. You've been very helpful to me. This case is gonna generate heat from a lot of different directions. I don't want anything getting out to the press that might jeopardize this case. I trust you completely, but you're still a rookie in this unit, and loose lips sink ships. You'd be amazed at what lengths reporters will go through to get a piece of information about a hot case. I've seen cases go down the tube because of media reports by unscrupulous reporters."

"So keep me informed and tell me to keep my mouth shut. I certainly wouldn't talk to the media about an ongoing investigation. Anyway, where did the crucifix come from?"

"It was in the dead boy's hand."

Confessions, Lies, and Secrets   *Stu Milisci*

"Well then you have your killer. Mr. Caruso said the crucifix looked exactly like the one Father Watson wears."

"Then maybe we should head over to the school right now and lock him up? Caruso couldn't know if it was Father Watson's. He said it looks like the one he wears."

"You're lead detective on the investigation so I'm not going to tell you how to run your case, but wouldn't the crucifix tend to incriminate Father Watson?"

"Moe, I know this makes the case look like a slam dunk, but I don't buy it yet. It seems too easy. The crucifix might have been planted at the crime scene by the real killer. We have to find out where Watson keeps it and who might have had access to it. I think we should have an interview with Father Watson before we go locking anybody up. I'll set up an appointment for tomorrow afternoon at the school and tell him to have the entire faculty there. I want to take a good look at everyone. There's another piece of evidence which may be as important to the case as the crucifix."

Moe's expression changed from annoyance to anticipation.

"And what might that be?"

A folding metal chair was recovered at the scene. The young boy seemed to have put up quite a struggle from the looks of the crime scene. I think the kid used the chair to try to ward off his attacker. It had a piece of scalp and some hair follicles on the bottom of one of the legs. I think Steven struck his attacker with the chair and took a little piece of his head from him. When we have everyone gathered together at the school tomorrow, I want you to walk around and see if you notice anyone with any kind of head wound. An injury should be to the right side of the scalp since Steven had a defensive wound to his right arm and would have had to use his left hand to strike a blow with the folding chair.

"Try not to be too conspicuous."

Confessions, Lies, and Secrets *Stu Milisci*

CHAPTER 16

More Evidence

When the two detectives returned to their office, Mike handed Moe the school yearbook he had retrieved from the school, which he had looked through earlier in the day.

"I want you to take a close look at this yearbook and tell me if you see anything which might help in this investigation. Start from the beginning and take a close look and let me know if you see anything interesting. Nothing specific, just anything that might be useful to this investigation."

"You gotta be kidding me. Right there on the third page is a picture of Father Watson wearing the crucifix around his neck."

"I got a message from a tech at the crime lab," Mike said as he shook his head. "They cleaned up the crucifix and were able to read an inscription etched on the back of it."

"What was written? Moe asked excitedly. "Does it prove the crucifix is Watson's?"

"The inscription is in Latin and it reads, 'Ad Maiorem Dei Gloriam', with a date 10/12/55. From my days long ago as an altar boy, I can translate the Latin to mean, 'To the greater glory of God'. That is the motto of the Jesuit order. I can only assume right now the date corresponds to when Watson was ordained. More evidence seeming to point to Father Watson as our killer. I tell you Moe, this is too coincidental to be real."

"Mike, we've limited our suspects, pretty much, to someone who was at the rectory on the night of the murder. You found a piece of evidence belonging to one of the possible suspects. I may be new at this, but it looks like a slam dunk to me."

"Moe I've been doing this a long time. This is your first homicide. If something looks or sounds too good to be true, they don't come this easily. This wasn't a spur of the moment act. This was well planned and thought out. I can't imagine anyone who planned this so well being careless enough to leave such an incriminating piece of evidence behind. No one discovered the body until many hours after the crime was committed which gave the perpetrator plenty of time to make sure there was nothing left behind at the scene. It also gave him plenty of time to go to Watson's room, snatch the crucifix, and come back and plant it at the scene."

Musto shifted gears and asked thoughtfully, "Did you notice during your initial interviews on the morning after the crime or in our follow up at the rectory if any of the faculty was left handed?"

"No. How's that important?"

"Steven Caruso had a defensive wound to his right forearm meaning, if his assailant was facing him, he was most likely left handed. Take a look at the written statements you assembled and check out who might be left handed."

"How in the hell can I determine that from written statements?"

"When right handed people write, their letters generally slant to the right. When left handed people write, their letters generally slant to the left. Let's look at those together."

After checking out the hand written statements, the two detectives determined three of the thirty-two faculty members were probably left handed. Father Watson was not one of them.

Mike began gathering everything pertaining to the investigation and told his partner, 'Time for a trip to the district attorneys' office to catch them up to speed on this case. I'm sure Shapiro is chomping at the bit for a collar and a quick conviction."

Confessions, Lies, and Secrets *Stu Milisci*

CHAPTER 17

The District Attorney

Harold Shapiro was the senior assistant district attorney for homicide cases in the Brooklyn District Attorneys' office. He had been an Assistant District Attorney for nearly twenty years and had forgone entering private practice for more money in hopes of one day becoming the elected District Attorney of Kings County. The sitting District Attorney was in his late 70s and having served many years, there was speculation he would soon retire. Shapiro had an excellent conviction record in noteworthy and highly publicized murder cases over the years, was well liked, and felt he would be a shoe- in when the old DA retired. Steven's murder had garnered enormous publicity generating pressure from the Mayor's office and the Archdiocese of New York to see closure. He figured such a high profile and public sentiment case could help get him elected.

Confessions, Lies, and Secrets   *Stu Milisci*

That pressure flowed down to the Police Commissioner, the Chief of Detectives, and, finally to the assigned detective, Mike Musto. Musto knew the evidence he had gathered so far clearly pointed to Father Watson as Steven's murderer, but he had a hunch the priest wasn't the killer. He got in touch with Harold Shapiro and bought him up to speed on what he had so far. He told Shapiro about his wanting to interview all the suspects at the rectory with a view to seeing if any of them had a wound to the head. He also told him of his theory the murderer was most likely left handed, and Father Watson wasn't one of the three faculty members who appeared to be left handed. Shapiro agreed to let Mike proceed with the interviews. He told him to give special attention to Father Watson since he was the lead suspect so far and told him to conduct the interviews quickly and then come into the DA's office to plan their next move. He told Mike he was allowing him the chance to look into the case further as a courtesy and would have demanded an immediate arrest if anyone else had been the lead detective in the case. Mike thanked the prosecutor and told him he'd get back to him when the interviews were completed.

* * * *

Shapiro felt he already had an iron clad case against Father Watson, but any new evidence would only strengthen his case and insure a conviction. He sensed Musto might have had some misgivings about Father Watson being the murderer, but he knew from here on out, he would control what happened next in this case.

CHAPTER 18

The Interviews

When the two detectives arrived at the rectory, those people who had been requested to be there were present and eager to cooperate. Thirty-two priests and seminarians were to be interviewed since they had been present at the rectory on the night of the crime. Detective Musto hadn't come to any suspicions about guilt or innocence during the initial interviews on the morning of the murder, so this was his opportunity to ask questions and size up people.

His questions were mostly a rehash of what had been asked before and all of the responses and alibis seemed to mirror what had been initially told to the Detective. While Mike was taking individual suspects to a private office for questioning, Moe walked among those waiting to be questioned and tried not to be too conspicuous looking for signs of any injuries to anyone's head. Mike's interviews and Moe's attempts to locate any injuries didn't produce anything new, but it gave Mike a chance to observe each suspect's behavior and demeanor

Confessions, Lies, and Secrets   *Stu Milisci*

while being questioned. This is often an investigator's best tool in creating suspects based on their reactions. Almost like a lie detector, without the polygraph machine, the body language and voice inflections of a suspect can tell a story. Mike didn't notice anything in anyone's behavior to make him suspicious, but he was able to find out Mr. Savino had been Steven's homeroom teacher and counselor and had a lot more access to Steven than any other faculty member. That fact alone made Mike put Savino one rung higher on his list of suspects, not to mention he had a full head of wavy, brown hair. What little hair Father Watson had was gray and cut very short.

    Savino was also left handed. He was the only left handed faculty member with a full head of dark brown hair. Two clues that made Savino a likely suspect.

CHAPTER 19

The Lead Suspect

The two detectives returned to their office following the interviews at the rectory.

"Well, Mike, did you get anymore leads based on the interviews?" Moe asked.

"Nothing that would break the case, but my feelings about Father Watson were reinforced by meeting him in person. I'd like to have him come into the office and talk to him one-on-one. He doesn't know about the crucifix yet, and I'm eager to see his reaction when we spring it on him. I'll set up an interview for tomorrow afternoon." Mike called the rectory and got the priest on the phone. "Father Watson, this is detective Musto, the lead detective investigating the murder of Steven Caruso."

"Yes, detective, I know who you are. How can I help you?"

"I'd like you to come to our office sometime tomorrow afternoon if possible. I'd like to ask you some questions about our investigation."

"I'll make myself available anytime you want. Would 4:00 o'clock be okay?"

"That would be fine, and Father, you might want to bring an attorney with you."

"Detective, I have done nothing wrong and I'll come alone."

"Your choice, Father. I'll see you tomorrow."

CHAPTER 20

Face To Face

Father Watson showed up at the 71st Detective office at four o'clock the next day. Detective Musto knew from past experience suspects with something to hide would usually not show up, show up late, or have an attorney with them. Father Watson was alone and on time, which added to Mike's impression of him being innocent.

After exchanging greetings, Detective Musto asked the priest to have a seat and began the interview. He asked the priest to give him a brief biography of his life in an effort to know him better. Father Watson told of his early childhood in Hell's Kitchen, his minor skirmishes with law enforcement, his military service in Pearl Harbor, his decision to enter the priesthood and his assignments and accomplishments since his ordination.

"Thank you, Father, that was very informative. It seems you and I have a lot in common. I also left school before graduating and enlisted to serve in World War II."

Confessions, Lies, and Secrets *Stu Milisci*

Mike had done many interviews with witnesses and suspects and individualized his approach depending on the person being interviewed. He felt with Father Watson, he would try to put him at ease and try to relate to him as an equal. Father Watson recognized what Mike was doing and appreciated his style since he probably would have done the same thing had their roles been reversed. Water and coffee were offered to the witness and politely refused. Mike then continued with his questioning after the two men exchanged some war stories.

"Now, Father, I'm going to show you something and ask you if you recognize it." Mike took out the photo of the crucifix and chain and placed it on the desk between the two of them never taking his eyes off Watson's face.

Father Watson momentarily seemed surprised to see the photo.

Detective Musto noticed the priest's reaction and thought it was genuine.

"Detective, that's a photo of my crucifix. How did it come to be in your possession?"

"When was the last time you remember seeing the crucifix?"

"The night of the murder of Steven Caruso. Mr. Shay awakened me at the rectory and told me what he had discovered at the cafeteria. I dressed quickly to get over there and noticed my crucifix wasn't on the night table next to my bed. I always leave it there while sleeping. I didn't pay much attention, thinking I might have knocked it off the table in my rush to get dressed. Obviously, I was in a hurry to go to the cafeteria."

"The crucifix was found in Steven's hand. If you look closely, you'll see one of the links on the chain is broken, as if it were pulled away from someone wearing it. It also has an inscription on the back in Latin and a date."

Father Watson moved forward in his chair. "The inscription translates as, 'To The Greater Glory of God', which is the motto of the Jesuit Order. The date is when I was ordained, but I suspect you already knew that."

"Father, you're very perceptive."

"As are you, detective. I guess, in a way, we're both in the perception business."

Both of these men realized they shouldn't underestimate one another.

"Did you report the crucifix missing to anyone?"

"Detective, as I'm sure you can imagine, a misplaced crucifix isn't something important in light of what had happened in the cafeteria. I didn't give it any thought, and felt it would turn up when my room was cleaned."

"Did this crucifix have any sentimental value to you? Any special significance?"

"Yes, this crucifix is the most valued material gift I have ever received." Father Watson then told Detective Musto the story of his ordination and the gift Father Rooney had given him.

"Father, I'm sure you can see what an important piece of evidence this is and how incriminating it is against you."

"Detective, I've told you how I lost or misplaced it. You can choose to believe me or not."

Confessions, Lies, and Secrets　　　　　　　*Stu Milisci*

Detective Musto leaned in a little closer to the priest. "Father, if our roles were reversed, what would you do?"

Up until this question, Father Watson had not hesitated with any of his answers. He paused, disdain crossing his face, and looked directly into the detective's eyes before responding. "Detective, if some lost soul came to me and told me he had given up on his faith and turned to me to restore it, I doubt I would come to you to ask for advice."

Mike leaned back a little in his chair. "You're right Father. I apologize. I'm sure you're aware of the amount of pressure from all sides this case has generated."

"Believe me, Detective, there's a lot of pressure coming at me from the Archdiocese. Are you going to arrest me based on this evidence?"

"I'm not going to arrest you now, but the District Attorney will have the final say about if and when an arrest will take place. My gut feeling is he'll either convene a Grand Jury or charge you with first degree murder, at which time you'll be arrested. For now, you're free to go and thank you for coming in."

The two men parted with mutual respect.

CHAPTER 21

Pressure

"Lock him up, Mike!"

Detectives Musto and Gold were in Assistant District Attorney Shapiro's office bringing him up to speed on the investigation. "Mr. Shapiro, I know how bad this looks for Father Watson, but my gut feeling tells me he didn't do this."

"Detective Musto, we don't prosecute cases based on gut feelings of lead detectives. We follow the evidence. The evidence in this case says this priest is a murderer."

"Mr. Shapiro, there's another piece of valuable evidence which points as clearly to Father Watson's innocence."

"What might that be, Detective?"

"The folding chair which was recovered at the scene of the crime. It had a hair follicle on one of the legs. I believe Steven struck his attacker in the head with this chair and took away a piece of his scalp. The hair was dark and thick. Father Watson wears his hair in a military style crew cut and it's almost totally gray. There are only three people I noticed during the interrogations we conducted at the school who were present at the rectory on the night of the crime who had hair that seemed to match the sample on the chair leg. One of them was Mr. Savino, who I like very much as a suspect. He's also the only one of the three who is left handed."

"Detective, the chair will be introduced as evidence at the trial. You're only to answer questions asked and not questions that aren't asked while testifying. Your theory about the attacker being left handed is just that—a theory. If the attacker was right handed and he came at Steven brandishing a knife in his right hand, Steven might have picked up that chair in his left hand and struck his assailant in the hand with the knife—his right hand. The murderer would then most likely have switched hands and Steven received the defensive wound to his right arm since the assailant now had the knife in his left hand."

Musto shifted in his chair, but did not speak.

Shapiro continued. "The defense will have a detailed list of the evidence. Let's leave it up to them to make an issue about the hair and scalp evidence. I'm not suggesting you perjure yourself while on the stand. I have prosecuted police officers and detectives for such testimony. I'm telling you not to offer any personal opinions about any evidence unless questioned about it. I don't need you to punch holes in this prosecution."

"Mr. Shapiro, I've never lied on the stand nor do I intend to start now. I have one of the best conviction rates in the department and I rely on legal tactics to get convictions. I use what I have available to me. I've lied to suspects during interrogations, but this is allowed and has proven to be very effective for me. I would never compromise my integrity for a conviction, unlike some other people I've known."

The ADA knew the detective's last remark was aimed at him and other members of his staff. ADA Shapiro and Detective Musto had worked many cases together and for the most part, got along well. Their goals were the same, to convict persons guilty of crime, but their tactics weren't always on the same track. When they agreed, they were on a first name basis. When they didn't, they weren't. Shapiro turned toward Moe.

"Detective Gold, if your partner refuses to make the arrest because of some gut feeling he has, you make the arrest. It wouldn't look good for someone other than the lead detective to make the arrest, but I want this man arrested and arraigned. There isn't a need to convene a Grand Jury. I'll make the charge and arraign him."

Shapiro returned his attention to Musto. "Did he have an attorney present when you interviewed him, detective?"

"No, he came in alone. He's a priest and I'm sure he can't afford an attorney. Judging by the signals coming from the Archdiocese, I doubt if the Cardinal will use any church money for his defense. He'll probably have to settle for legal aide to represent him."

"Great. That should make the case even easier. I don't want any plea bargaining here. This is a capital case and the public will demand capital punishment for this heinous crime. This kind of conduct has been going on for a long time among members of the clergy. Until now, there has never been a conviction. I intend to change that with this case."

Confessions, Lies, and Secrets   *Stu Milisci*

    Musto turned away from Shapiro with a furtive look. "I'm the lead detective, and I'll make the arrest, as much as I think he's not the person who did this. I've been around long enough to know what my responsibilities are, but if you convict an innocent man, it's on your conscience."
    "The ball is out of your court, Detective, from now on, it's my ball game."

CHAPTER 22

An Arrest

Detective Musto returned to his office and called Father Watson at the rectory. "Father Watson, I just returned from the District Attorney's office and I have been ordered to arrest you for the murder of Steven Caruso. I would like you to surrender to me at my office this afternoon. The other alternative is for me to arrest you at the rectory, which I'm sure you'd prefer not to happen. You may bring an attorney with you if you wish. The choice is yours."

"Detective, I'm not surprised by your call. I've been expecting it. I appreciate you giving me the opportunity to come in and surrender on my own. I don't have an attorney nor can I afford one. I'ill surrender later this afternoon as soon as I clear up some details at the school."

Later in the afternoon, Father Watson appeared at the Detective Squad's office and was placed under arrest. He was photographed, fingerprinted, processed and charged with murder in the death of Steven Caruso. Detectives

Musto and Gold then escorted him to Criminal Court on Schermerhorn Street in downtown Brooklyn to be arraigned. The soon to be former priest pleaded "Not guilty" and was remanded to the jail at Rikers Island without bail. A trial date was set for early in the summer and Father Watson was placed in a cell awaiting transport to Rikers. Once he arrived at Rikers, he was issued an orange jump suit, given a toothbrush and other toiletries and placed in a receiving cell with twenty other prisoners.

CHAPTER 23

The Church

As soon as Cardinal Walsh, the prelate of the diocese, saw the headlines in the morning papers about a Jesuit priest assigned to his diocese being arrested for murder, he set the wheels in motion to have this priest dismissed from the priesthood or defrocked as it is commonly referred to by non members of the clergy. Cardinal Walsh certainly had the grounds to do this since Cannon Law was explicit that "a cleric can be dismissed from the clerical state if he commits an offense against the Sixth Commandment with a minor under the age of sixteen."

Cardinal Walsh was a member of the Dominican order and a student of church history. He had no love for the Jesuits and thought them to be elitists. He was aware the Jesuits had been driven from many European nations during the sixteenth century and were accused of heresy. He felt they never should have been allowed back.

Confessions, Lies, and Secrets   *Stu Milisci*

  The Catholic Church had been criticized globally for not taking decisive action when allegations of sexual abuse were being directed against priests. Some Cardinals who were slow to respond or tried to cover up these allegations were criticized and reassigned. Cardinal Walsh was not going to allow this to happen to him.

  He saw this as an opportunity to show the church took these hideous crimes seriously and these offenses would not be tolerated in his diocese. They would be punished to the fullest extent possible. He would show no sympathy for the accused priest even though he hadn't even come to trial yet, nor would he provide any church funds for his defense. He hoped by the time the trial started, Andrew Watson would no longer be a priest. He petitioned the Vatican to have Watson dismissed from the clerical state (defrocked) as quickly as possible, so any references to him at trial as a priest would be challenged since he would no longer be a priest. The Vatican was quick and firm in their response and immediately began the process to have Father Watson defrocked.

  Whatever happened in a criminal court of law had no bearing on how Cardinal Walsh and the Catholic Church would handle this situation.

CHAPTER 24

The Defense Attorney

Anna Ruiz was an attractive, ambitious, intelligent young attorney of Puerto Rican ancestry. She resembled the up and coming Puerto Rican movie star Rita Moreno, but had no discernible accent. Her parents migrated to the United States before she was born and settled on the Upper East Side of Manhattan. The neighborhood was known as Spanish Harlem due to the influx of many people from their island habitat. She received her primary and secondary education courtesy of the New York City Board of Education. She excelled in academics and in high school was the captain of the debate team, editor of the school newspaper, and valedictorian of her graduating class.

Affirmative action was a new concept, which was based on the premise that many minorities hadn't been given a fair shake when it came to opportunities for higher education and job placement. As a female of Puerto Rican ancestry, Anna Ruiz could have been the poster child for affirmative action. After high school, she was accepted at Hunter College on a full scholarship where she continued to be the outstanding student and community activist she had proved herself to be in high school. She was accepted into New York Law School, also on a full scholarship, where she received her Law Degree and later passed the bar exam on her first attempt with one of the highest scores ever recorded. Anna could have easily gotten a job as an associate attorney in any one of a number of prestigious law firms in New York City, but she chose to practice criminal law and took a job with the Public Defenders' Office. She felt this was a good first step to lead her down the path she would travel with hopes of being appointed to a judgeship. She would devote herself to defending indigent minorities and championing the causes of the liberal agenda.

  The Public Defenders Office was aware of the publicity and public outcry the murder of Steven Caruso had generated. While it was their job to offer the best defense possible in cases assigned to their office, often this meant negotiating a plea bargain with the prosecutor in order to clear both of their calendars while making it appear justice was still done. The prosecution would be credited with a conviction and the defendant would get a reduced sentence or, sometimes, a suspended sentence and serve no jail time at all. They knew there would be no plea bargaining in a capital case which caused so much outrage and anger in the community. The DA'S office wouldn't make any kind of a deal that would incur the wrath of the public. The case was given to one of their least senior attorneys, Anna Ruiz.

Anna was not too surprised the case was given to her to defend. She knew her office would also have to answer to the court of public opinion if Andy Watson wasn't convicted. From the outset, she decided she would offer only an adequate defense in the case making it appear Watson was given a fair trial, but convicted none the less. She was okay with this, knowing she would be seen by both sides as a team player and not make enemies on either side. The fact that Andy Watson might not have been guilty didn't matter to her. She had a goal in life and would allow nothing to stand in the way of her reaching it. If it meant an innocent man was convicted, and even executed, she lacked the morality, conscience, and compassion to allow this to bother her. She could rationalize it was the fault of the police, who arrested him, the prosecution who charged him, and the jury who convicted him. It had nothing to do with her.

Confessions, Lies, and Secrets   *Stu Milisci*

CHAPTER 25

The Press

Jack Ryan had been a crime reporter for the Daily News since the days of Al Capone, Meyer Lansky, Lucky Luciano, and Elliot Ness. His excellent research, investigative ability and tremendous network of informants within the DA's office, the police department and on the street, had proven so good he was awarded a Pulitzer Prize in journalism several years before the trial of Andy Watson. He, like Detective Musto, had developed a sixth sense which gave him the ability to size people up during interviews by their body language, inability to look the interviewer in the eye, and general composure.

    He had followed the story of Steven Caruso's murder in his paper and other sources of media closely and had written several articles about the incident himself. While he wasn't given the opportunity to interview Andy Watson in jail prior to the trial, he did interview many who would be called as witnesses during the trial. They all painted a picture of Father Watson as a caring and competent educator and minister to the people of his parish. Ryan was aware the entire case seemed to hinge on the crucifix, which was recovered in the dead boy's hand. He also felt, as did Detective Musto, that the evidence could have been planted at the crime scene, planted by someone who may have been the actual killer. He didn't interview Detective Musto, but unnamed sources within the Police Department made Ryan aware of the detective's misgivings about the crucifix. He had written many articles about defendants who he felt were innocent of the charges brought against them. Ryan was right on so many occasions he had developed a strong following among the public. He and Detective Musto also agreed it was better to have ten guilty men go free than to have one innocent person convicted of a crime he didn't commit. Most criminals were recidivists, and would likely be arrested again for some future crime, convicted, and sent to prison anyway.

So as the trial date neared, Jack Ryan took a very keen interest in a case he knew had gotten worldwide publicity. He was sure enough of himself, and his following, that he wrote several articles proclaiming the fact that Andrew Watson could very well be innocent. He included in these articles the Catholic Church's past indifference to allegations of sexual abuse by members of the clergy and their desire to make an example of Andy Watson in this case.

He also doubted if Andy Watson could get a fair trial due to all the adverse publicity from the media including his own paper. He suggested a change of venue would be more fair to the defendant and give him a better chance for an acquittal.

Confessions, Lies, and Secrets   *Stu Milisci*

CHAPTER 26

The Judge

Leon Glass had been very active in politics as a young prosecutor working in the Kings County District Attorney's Office. He was also an ambitious attorney with a high conviction rate. His reward for his political support and his zeal as a prosecutor came in the form of being appointed a criminal court judge in the same county more than twenty years prior to the Watson trial. He had the reputation of being a "Hanging Judge," since most of the capital cases he presided over resulted in convictions. This wound up getting the guilty party a one way ticket to the electric chair. He was a God fearing zealot who liked to quote the bible in his decisions and sentencing. He was a natural choice to preside over such a notable and publicized capital case, which had engendered so much hatred for the accused by the community.

There were many times the judge's Manhattan Beach home in a trendy neighborhood in the southern tip of

Brooklyn would have a police car parked out front because the judge had received many death threats. Rather than being frightened by these threats, Judge Glass welcomed them since he felt they showed how tough he was and how he refused to be intimidated by low life criminals. None of the cops assigned to guard his house ever remember being offered a glass of water or a cup of coffee.

So a trial date was set, summonses were sent out to prospective jurors, and the prosecutor and defense attorney were assigned. It would be ADA Shapiro for the prosecution, and Anna Ruiz for the defense.

Thirty prospective jurors, twelve of whom would be selected, were led into court to start the process of "voir dire" (a French term meaning to speak the truth). The judge, the prosecutor, and the defense attorney could ask any and all prospective jurors a series of questions to determine if they had any prejudices or preconceived feelings about guilt or innocence The jurors were also asked if they supported capital punishment. Either side could have a prospective juror dismissed if they appeared to be disqualified to serve. They also had the right to dismiss a juror without cause if they felt the juror might be prejudicial to their case.

Questions were asked and answers were given. Neither the prosecution nor the defense challenged any jurors. The presiding judge impaneled the jury of twelve with two alternates who would serve only if one of the original jurors was unable to continue due to health reasons or any other situation which the judge felt was grounds for dismissal of a juror.

The jury consisted of eight men and four women. Six of the jurors were Catholics, four of whom had gone to Catholic grammar schools. None of the jurors were opposed to the death penalty in capital offenses.

The prosecution had notified the defense of all the evidence they had available, all the exhibits they would enter, and the names of all the witnesses they would call upon to testify. The physical evidence included the murder weapon, a knife taken from the cafeteria, a gold crucifix and chain, which had been taken from the victims right hand at the crime scene, and a metal folding chair, also taken from the cafeteria. There was also a series of photographs and charts prepared by the Crime Scene Unit depicting the scene as it appeared shortly after the crime had been completed. There were several medical documents entered into evidence which the pathologist who performed the autopsy on Steven Caruso, would have to explain to the jury when he testified because they were not submitted in laymen's terms and had no meaning whatsoever to the jury the way they were presented.

The prosecution's witness list was extensive, but didn't include three names the prosecution team would have liked to give testimony. The Carusos had pleaded with the ADA not to have to be present at the trial citing the fact it would have been too emotional for them. They chose to sit it out at home and let the jury decide the guilt or innocence of Andrew Watson. They had a strong belief Andrew Watson wasn't guilty of murdering their son and didn't want to be part of a system that convicted a man they thought to be innocent. ADA Shapiro felt his case was strong enough without needing the testimony of the

Carusos, and he didn't want witnesses who felt the defendant might have been innocent to testify. So he left them off the witness list.

He also would have liked to have Father Rooney present in court to testify to the fact he had given Andrew Watson the gold chain and crucifix, but it was determined he was too old and his health too poor for him to appear in court. Shapiro felt if the jury saw Father Rooney, they would feel empathetic toward the old man and felt that would bolster his case. Both sides agreed, and the judge ruled his testimony could be shown to the jury by means of a recorded deposition which ADA Shapiro had taken before the trial started.

CHAPTER 27

The Trial

Assistant District Attorney Shapiro addressed the jury with his opening statement. He was dressed in a Brooks Brother's gray, three-button suit with a maroon shadow stripe running through it and a matching vest. Although he was small in stature, he had charisma and an air of confidence and quickly had the jury's attention.

He told the jury the prosecution would produce witnesses and evidence that would leave no doubt in their minds Andrew Watson was guilty of murdering Steven Caruso. He related the gruesome details of how the dead boy's body had been discovered in the cafeteria to which Andrew Watson had access. He told of finding the chain and crucifix in the dead boy's hand and how several witnesses would testify to the fact that crucifix belonged to Andrew Watson and they had seen him wearing it daily. He assured them although this physical evidence may only be circumstantial, often times convictions were obtained from circumstantial evidence when that evidence was so compelling, a crime really did happen the way it appeared. He would cite many such cases as the trial progressed. He stated the circumstantial evidence in this case met that requirement. No reasonable doubt would be left in the mind of any juror regarding Andrew Watson's guilt.

CHAPTER 28

For The Defense

Anna Ruiz was next to address the jury with her opening statement. She wore a fashionable pants suit and her long dark hair was fastened in a bun atop her head. Like ADA Shapiro, Anna Ruiz was small in stature, but she didn't project the kind of confidence the ADA did. She was only twenty-four years old and looked even younger. She appeared to be frightened and in over her head, and the jury took notice of this.

She told the jury the case against her client rested solely on one piece of circumstantial evidence, the chain and crucifix. While she readily admitted these items belonged to Andrew Watson, she planted a seed of doubt in the jurors' minds as to other possible ways that one piece of evidence could have been found at the crime scene. She told the members of the jury the real killer, whoever that might be, could easily have gotten the crucifix from Andrew Watson and planted it at the scene to incriminate him.

    Andrew Watson slept in an unlocked room and didn't wear the crucifix while he slept. Someone could have gone into his room while he was asleep and stolen the crucifix. Someone who also had access to the cafeteria. She told the jury thirty-two people had slept at the rectory on the night of Steven's murder and numerous other people could have gotten into the school. She said these facts created more than enough reasonable doubt to acquit Andrew Watson of all charges.

CHAPTER 29

Testimony

The first witness called to the stand by the prosecution was the first uniformed officer to arrive on the scene the morning after the murder. Responding to ADA Shapiro's questions, he explained to the jury what he saw when he arrived, how he taped off the entire cafeteria as a crime scene, and his notification to the dispatcher to have a detective unit respond to begin an investigation. He also described how the deceased's family was personally notified and their reactions when told of their son's murder.

He stated the parents had no idea what time their son had left the house or where he had gone. The officer testified when he notified the parents in the morning of what had taken place in the cafeteria, it was the first they realized their son wasn't home the previous night.

During her cross examination of this witness, Ms. Ruiz asked only one question of the officer. She asked if he had noticed anything in the deceased's hands. The witness said he had not.

The next witness called to testify by ADA Shapiro was the custodian, Sean Shay. He related how he had gone to the cafeteria on the morning after the murder, what he had discovered when he got there, and his notification to Father Watson.

ADA Shapiro: "Mr. Shay, while the court is aware of the fact Andrew Watson was an ordained priest at the time of the incident, he no longer holds that position. You may refer to him as Mr. Watson, Andrew Watson or plain Andy, but you will not refer to him as 'Father' Watson'."

After admonishing the witness about his reference to the defendant as a priest, ADA Shapiro asked him a few more questions and told Anna Ruiz he was now her witness.

Anna Ruiz asked Sean Shay the same question she had asked the previous witness, and she got the same response, he had not seen anything in Steven's Caruso's hands. Ms. Ruiz was trying to plant a seed of doubt in the minds of the jurors as to when and how the crucifix wound up in the hand of the victim.

Anna Ruiz: "Mr. Shay, what time did you arrive at the cafeteria on the morning of May 13th?"

Mr. Shay: "About 6:30 a.m.."

Anna Ruiz: "Upon entering the cafeteria, what did you see?"

Mr.Shay: "I saw what appeared to be the body of a young boy lying on the cafeteria floor in a pool of blood."

Anna Ruiz: "What action did you take after seeing what you saw?"

Mr. Shay: "I went to the rectory to notify the pastor."

Anna Ruiz: "What condition was the pastor in when you got to his room?"

Mr. Shay: "He was asleep."

Anna Ruiz: "Could you tell the jury what Andrew Watson did when you told him what you had discovered in the cafeteria?"

Mr. Shay: "He got dressed and we left for the cafeteria."

Anna Ruiz: " Now, Mr. Shay, this is very important. So think back and try to recall if Andrew Watson took any objects from the night stand next to his bed."

Mr. Shay: "Yes, he did."

Anna Ruiz: "Do you remember what those objects were?"

Mr. Shay: "He took a pair of eyeglasses and a wrist watch."

Anna Ruiz: "Did Andrew Watson say anything to you about something missing from the nightstand?"

Mr. Shay: "No, he didn't, but he looked around on the floor at the base of the nightstand as if something was missing."

ADA Shapiro stood and offered an objection, "Your Honor that response is an opinion on the part of the witness."

Judge Glass, "Overruled. The witness is testifying to what he actually saw."

Confessions, Lies, and Secrets　　　　　　　　*Stu Milisci*

Anna Ruiz: "Was Watson wearing a crucifix around his neck when the two of you left his room to go back to the cafeteria?"

Mr. Shay: "I'm sorry. I don't remember."

Anna Ruiz: "Thank you for your testimony. I have no further questions for this witness."

Judge Glass: "Thank you, Mr. Shay. You may be excused."

CHAPTER 30

Detective Musto

The next witness called to testify by the prosecution was Detective Mike Musto.

  Shapiro and Musto were well known to each other and might even have been friends, although they didn't socialize together. They had worked many cases together and Musto had testified for the prosecution in many cases for which Shapiro had gotten convictions. They were on the same side, teammates one could speculate, but Shapiro knew Musto had grave misgivings about this case. He also knew Musto had a lot of experience testifying and knew how to appeal to a jury. He wasn't going to go easy on Musto and allow him to sway the jury into thinking Watson might be innocent.

  ADA Shapiro: "How did you come to respond to the crime scene on the morning of May 13th, 1963?"

  Det. Musto: "I received a phone call at my home from the dispatcher."

ADA Shapiro: "Were you on or off duty at the time?"

Det. Musto: "It was my scheduled day off. I was off duty."

ADA Shapiro: "Could you explain to the jury why you would be called at home on your day off to respond to the scene of a crime?"

Det. Musto: "In crimes of a serious nature, like a homicide, the department likes to assign more senior detectives to the investigation, especially when it appears the crime will cause a lot of public outcry."

ADA Shapiro: "Could you tell the jury what you found when you arrived at the scene and your observations of the crime scene."

Det. Musto: "I arrived at the cafeteria of the school at approximately 8:07 a.m.. There were two uniformed police officers at the scene, a team from the crime scene unit, as well as the civilian custodian of the school, Sean Shay, and the headmaster and parish pastor, Andrew Watson. There was a teenaged boy, who appeared to be dead, on the floor of the cafeteria.

ADA Shapiro: "What made you suspect the boy was dead?"

Det. Musto: "I've been investigating homicides for many years and through my training, experience, and expertise, it was obvious to me the boy was lifeless. Besides, the paramedics had arrived and left prior to my getting to the scene and they had pronounced him dead."

ADA Shapiro: "Did you notice anything of any evidentiary value?"

Det. Musto: " Several things. I saw a butcher knife on the floor in close proximity to the body, which was taken from the scene by the crime lab technicians, tested, and has been entered into evidence in this case. Upon further examination by the criminal lab and the Medical Examiner it was determined this knife was the murder weapon. I saw an overturned folding metal chair which appeared to have a piece of skin and some hair strands attached to one of the legs, and a yellow colored chain and crucifix which was recovered from the deceased's right hand. These items were also entered into evidence."

ADA Shapiro: "What was the significance of the chair and the crucifix?"

Det. Musto: "Since the chair had what seemed to be skin and hair on the bottom of one of it's legs, I surmised it may have been used by the victim in an attempt to ward off his attacker."

ADA Shapiro: "So you're saying you thought young Steven Caruso may have struck his attacker with that chair?"

Det. Musto: "Correct."

ADA Shapiro: "What value did you place on the chain and crucifix?"

Det.Musto: "Since it was recovered in the victim's hand, it's possible he pulled it from the attacker's neck during the struggle. It's also possible the real killer put it there to place suspicion on someone else when it was discovered who owned the crucifix."

That was the type of testimony Shapiro feared Musto would give in an attempt to place doubt in the minds of the jurors. Shapiro had to think fast and lessen its effect on the jurors.

ADA Shapiro: "Detective, please just testify to the evidence and the facts and don't include your personal opinions in this courtroom. At some point after you left the crime scene, did you discover who the crucifix belonged to?"

Det Musto: "I did"

ADA Shapiro: "Would you please tell the court how you made that discovery and who was the owner of this incriminating piece of evidence."

Det. Musto: "I went to the residence of Steven Caruso to interview his parents later in the day. I showed a photo of the crucifix to Mr. Caruso and asked him if he recognized it as belonging to his son. He told me it wasn't his son's crucifix, but he had seen Andrew Watson wearing that crucifix every time he had occasion to be in his presence. Andrew Watson also told me it was his crucifix when I interviewed him at my office several days later."

ADA Shapiro: "Did Andrew Watson offer you any kind of excuse as to how his crucifix wound up in the hand of a dead boy in the cafeteria of his school?

Det. Musto: "He told me he always takes off the chain and crucifix upon retiring and places them on a nightstand next to his bed. He said when he was notified by Mr. Shay about what happened in the cafeteria, he couldn't find the crucifix where he usually left it but, in light of what had happened, he assumed he misplaced it or knocked it off the nightstand in his hurry to get dressed to go to the cafeteria."

Shapiro realized he had reopened a door, which he just slammed shut by asking Musto if Watson had told him how he had misplaced the crucifix. He had enough faith in the jurors to speculate they would realize this would be the exact type of excuse Watson would make for the crucifix to be missing from his night table.

ADA Shapiro then asked the judge if he could approach the witness in order to show him a piece of evidence. The judge allowed him to approach the witness and Shapiro handed the chain and crucifix to Detective Musto.

ADA Shapiro: "Detective, is this chain and crucifix marked prosecution exhibit "C" the same crucifix that was recovered in Steven Caruso's hand?"

Det. Musto: "It is."

ADA Shapiro: "Take a close look at it and tell the court if there appears to be any damage to the chain."

Detective Musto looked at the chain for the sake of the jury. He had seen the broken link many times before and knew where this line of questioning was headed.

Det. Musto: "One of the links is broken."

ADA Shapiro: "Detective, is it not *reasonable* to assume, since the chain and crucifix were found in Steven's hand and since the chain was broken, is it not *reasonable* to assume Steven grabbed the chain while he was being attacked and ripped it from his attacker's neck?"

Det.Musto: "That's one possible explanation."

ADA Shapiro: "Thank you, detective. I have no more questions at this time. He's your witness. Counselor."

Shapiro hadn't given Detective Musto time to offer any other possible explanation.

Ms. Ruiz: "Detective Musto, you were about to offer an alternative as to how the crucifix may have been in the hand of the deceased."

ADA Shapiro: "Objection. Calls for an opinion on the part of the witness."

Judge Glass: "Sustained."

Ms. Ruiz: "Detective Musto you testified it was *reasonable* Steven had ripped the crucifix from his attacker's neck while being attacked. What other possible explanations could there be for the chain being broken?"

ADA Shapiro: "Objection, same grounds."

Judge Glass: "Same ruling."

Ms. Ruiz: "I have no further questions for this witness at this time."

Judge Glass: "Detective, thank you for your testimony. You may step down."

Anna Ruiz was aware of the evidence the prosecution had offered in the case. While evidence presented by the prosecution usually serves to strengthen their case, the defense can often use any evidence in the case to their advantage. Anna knew from observation the strands of dark brown hair on the leg of the chair recovered at the crime scene didn't match Andrew Watson's thinning gray hair. She also realized, since Steven had a defensive wound to his right arm, his attacker was most likely left handed and Watson was right handed.

The prosecution didn't make either of these facts known to the jury since they would seem to help the accused, but Anna Ruiz was aware of their value to the defense. Ordinarily, if she was really looking to present the best defense possible, she would have found a way to make the jury aware of these important holes in the prosecution's case, but she didn't want her client to be acquitted. If she won Watson's release, she would forever be known as the attorney who won freedom for a man the entire community wanted to be convicted.

She was convinced she had offered an adequate defense, and Watson would probably be convicted. She didn't want to take a chance of having him acquitted. She also realized the weaker the defense appeared to be, the stronger the argument would be for an appeal if there were a conviction. She hoped by that time, public outrage would have died down and a different attorney would handle the appeal.

Confessions, Lies, and Secrets   *Stu Milisci*

CHAPTER 31

More Testimony

The next witness called to the stand by the prosecution was the pathologist from the Medical Examiner's Office who had performed the autopsy on Steven Caruso.

After establishing himself as an expert witness based on his training, education, and experience, he testified the deceased had received sixteen stab wounds to the neck and upper torso, including one wound to the right forearm, which appeared to be a defensive wound.

He went into great detail about the placement of the wounds, the depth of each stab and stated unequivocally the cause of death was exsanguination due to multiple stab wounds. He testified it would have taken about ten minutes for the victim to die and the time of death was between 10:30 p.m. and midnight on May 12th.

He identified the knife recovered at the scene by the crime scene technicians and placed into evidence as being the murder weapon. He produced charts and graphs, which left no doubt in anyone's mind Steven Caruso was stabbed to death in a brutal fashion. He explained all the evidence, which had been introduced to the satisfaction of the jury.

Ms. Ruiz declined to ask any questions of this witness on cross examination as she felt nothing he could possibly testify to would be of any help to her defendant.

Several other witnesses were called to testify by the prosecution. They all testified to seeing Andrew Watson wearing the gold chain and crucifix whenever they were in his presence. The recorded video deposition of Father Rooney was shown to the jury and entered as an exhibit for the prosecution. In it the old priest related how he had given the crucifix to Andrew Watson upon his ordination and the significance of the inscription he had engraved on the back of it. It was established beyond any reasonable doubt the crucifix and chain were the property of Andrew Watson.

After the prosecution called all their witnesses and rested, Ms. Ruiz called several witnesses to the stand who basically stated they knew Andrew Watson to be a person of outstanding character. They cited his achievements as a Chaplain's Assistant during the war, as a teacher, headmaster, and parish pastor. Shapiro passed on cross examination of any of these defense witnesses. Both sides rested and court was recessed to the following morning at which time both sides would give their closing arguments.

CHAPTER 32

Closing Arguments

ADA Shapiro was the first to give his closing argument. He stood in front of the jury clad in another three-piece Brooks Brothers suit looking as if he had come from central casting.

"Ladies and gentlemen of the jury," he began, "I want to thank you, first and foremost, for your service. I have seen that you have been very attentive during this trial. I have seen many of you taking notes during testimony and I'm sure you will reach the proper verdict in this case.

"You have heard testimony from witnesses depicting Andrew Watson as a dedicated teacher and priest, but it is the abuse of his power in each of these roles that he used in the commission of this heinous murder. He took advantage of his position to intimidate the victim and other students at the school. He used corporal punishment, intimidation and deceit to become a despot with no restrictions to his power and oppressiveness. We send our children to school and expect they're in a safe environment, but, in this case, school was probably the least safe place Steven Caruso could have been. We expect those we entrust with our children to be caring, compassionate educators, but Andrew Watson was neither caring nor compassionate. While no one has suggested a motive, and that is not necessary for a conviction, we can only imagine the ugly circumstances which led to this despicable crime.

"The defense will argue this case is based on circumstantial evidence and ask you for a verdict of not guilty. Witness after witness testified the key piece of evidence, the crucifix, belonged to Andrew Watson. He was seen wearing it all the time. We even showed dear Father Rooney telling us how he had given the crucifix to Andrew Watson as a gift upon his ordination. There is no doubt. The crucifix is his and it was found in the victim's hand. This may be circumstantial evidence, but it's so compelling it establishes proof beyond any *reasonable* doubt as to the guilt of the defendant. I have cited numerous other cases establishing precedence for convictions based on circumstantial evidence.

"Ladies and gentlemen of the jury, I ask you to give justice to Steven Caruso. I ask you to give justice to his family. I ask you to convict Andrew Watson of murder in the first degree."

CHAPTER 33

The Defense Takes Its Turn

Ms. Ruiz stood before the jury to deliver her closing argument looking much the same as she had during her opening statement; wearing a pants suit, comfortable two inch wedges, and her long dark hair once again stacked in a bun atop her head.

She appeared much more confident now, than at the beginning of the trial. In fact, she was more at ease. Happy it would soon be over, a guilty verdict would be obtained by the prosecution, and she could go on with her life and her career without having made any enemies.

While she was reasonably confident Andrew Watson would be convicted and she wouldn't be viewed as not having presented a reasonable defense, she started questioning herself about whether or not she could have gotten him acquitted if she had put forth her best effort. This wasn't because she felt any kind of guilt or misgivings for a possibly innocent man being executed for a crime he didn't commit. She didn't know if Andrew Watson was guilty or innocent. Nor did she care. She was very competitive by nature and had gotten used to being successful in almost everything she did. Now she was going out of her way to fail in providing the kind of defense she felt sure would have won this case in favor of Andrew Watson. She decided to give a convincing and compelling closing argument. While she realized it was probably too little too late to do Watson any good, her pride compelled her to do something outstanding to finish up this trial.

"Ladies and gentlemen of the jury, I would also like to thank you for your attentiveness and tell you, although I don't have as much trial experience as my more seasoned adversary, I have come to feel very comfortable in this courtroom thanks in no small part to the professionalism you have all displayed."

"Andrew Watson gave up the secular life and devoted himself to God's work knowing well what sacrifices he'd have to make to devote his life to the education of our youth and the salvation of our multitudes. Jesuit priests take vows of chastity, poverty, and obedience. Think about that for a minute. They give up everything most people strive for all their lives. No family, no material possessions and very little say in where they live, how long they stay in one place or where they'll be told to go next.

Witness after witness came up to this stand and testified Andrew Watson was an excellent educator, an exemplary administrator, and a caring and compassionate pastor.

Confessions, Lies, and Secrets   *Stu Milisci*

    Recently, the Catholic Church has been rocked by a number of serious allegations regarding pedophiles among their ranks. None of these allegations have been proven in a court of law, but payments have been made to some of the claimants seeming to indicate perhaps there may be some truth to many of these allegations. Andrew Watson had been a priest for quite some time and there was never even a hint of any scandal regarding his behavior. Oh, he may have been a little rough on some of the boys, but sometimes those of us who are placed in a position of authority have to be a little rough.

    Because of these recent allegations against the church; the police, the church, and the public were in a rush to judgment for an arrest, a conviction, and punishment which would be swift and severe. No other possible suspects were thought about or investigated. Andrew Watson seemed to fit the bill, so he was arrested and stands before you an innocent man wrongfully accused of a crime he did not commit.

    The crucifix that was discovered in Steven Caruso's hand is Andrew Watson's. We do not deny that fact, but as soon as the investigating detective tried to offer an alternative as to how it got there, the prosecution objected. What that qualified detective might have told you is that on the night of this dastardly crime, thirty-two people were sleeping at the rectory. Thirty- two people who had access to the cafeteria. Any one of them could have entered Andrew Watson's room while he was asleep and removed the crucifix. What better way to make someone appear to be suspicious, than to place a personal item belonging to him at the crime scene?

There were no eye witnesses. There were no fingerprints. I ask you to think about that as you deliberate. Keep in mind this crucifix, this one piece of circumstantial evidence, is the most important item in the prosecution's arsenal. What of another piece of evidence? You have all seen the chair, which Steven probably struck his assailant with. I'm certain you could not help but notice the hair follicles on the leg of the chair were dark and thick. The defendant's hair is thin, short, and gray. Those hairs obviously didn't come from Andrew Watson. Is it not *reasonable* to suggest the real killer took this crucifix from Andrew Watson's night table where he kept it when he slept and planted it at the crime scene? If that is the only piece of evidence the prosecution has, if that is their entire case, and you agree it's *reasonable* someone other than Andrew Watson could have come into possession of that crucifix and placed it in Steven's hand, then you must find Andrew Watson innocent of all charges.

Thank you again for your attention."

CHAPTER 34

Jury Deliberations

After both attorneys finished their closing arguments, Judge Glass gave the jury its instructions. He advised them of all the elements necessary for a conviction for first degree murder and had them retire to the jury room to deliberate and reach a verdict. He told them if they had any questions, they should write them down on a piece of paper and have the bailiff take them to the judge for clarification. No pieces of paper were brought to the judge while the jury deliberated.

    Court stood in recess and most of the people present left to have lunch. Reporter Jack Ryan had been present at the trial since the first day, and had written several articles covering the case. He approached Ms. Ruiz as she was leaving the courtroom and asked if he could interview her. Never being someone who shied away from publicity, since she felt her name in the papers would help her career, she agreed to answer a few questions.

Ryan: "I like the way you got the fact the crucifix could have been planted, into the record after the prosecutor objected to Detective Musto's attempt to introduce it on direct testimony."

Ms. Ruiz: "The whole case rests on this one piece of circumstantial evidence. If the jury is left with a reasonable doubt how that crucifix wound up at the crime scene, they have to find the defendant not guilty."

Ryan: "Did you get the impression from Detective Musto's attempt to offer an alternative way of placing the crucifix at the scene, that he thinks Watson could be innocent?"

Ms. Ruiz: "It's obvious you have the same impression if you're asking me that question. I can only hope the jury felt the same way. It certainly helps my case if the jury senses the lead investigating detective thinks the defendant isn't guilty. I really have to go now, but I'll see you in the courtroom when the jury reaches a verdict."

Ms. Ruiz didn't want to say anything to this reporter that would make it seem as if she was hoping for a conviction of her client in this case. She wanted it to appear she had presented a good case and the jury just found for the State.

Ryan: "Thank you for the interview, and good luck. I've been covering crime stories and courtroom proceedings for a long time and I've been an advocate for the innocent on many occasions. Based on the evidence and facts in this particular case, I don't think the jury should convict. There's been so much adverse publicity, I doubt an objective jury could have been found, and that lessens the chances of your prevailing."

They shook hands and went their separate ways.

CHAPTER 35

Has The Jury Reached A Verdict?

Shortly after most of the spectators returned from lunch, the bailiff entered the courtroom and told the judge the jury had reached a verdict. They had only deliberated for three hours, which didn't look good for the defense. The judge had the jury brought back into the courtroom. After they were all seated, the judge told the defendant to stand while the verdict was rendered. The jury found Andrew Watson guilty of the most serious crime with which he had been charged, murder in the first degree.

      The courtroom erupted as most of the spectators started to applaud. The judge called for order in the court, admonished the spectators and threatened to have the courtroom cleared. Everyone quieted down and took their seats. Watson sat as well, displaying no emotion at all, which was consistent with his demeanor during the entire trial. The judge asked the prosecutor and defense attorney if either of them had any objection to the sentence being declared there and then.

Ordinarily, there would be a probation report done on the newly convicted felon prior to sentencing, but since the conviction was for a capital offense, it was a forgone conclusion what the sentence was going to be. Neither side objected and the judge didn't disappoint those in attendance with his sentence. He ordered the defendant to stand while the sentence was rendered.

Judge Glass, "Andrew Watson, you have been found guilty of first degree murder by a jury of your peers. While any murder, by virtue of the act alone, is a despicable and heinous crime, the crime you have committed rises to a level I have rarely witnessed from my many years on the bench.

"You have been given the opportunity to educate young men, and not only did you fail in that responsibility, you took advantage of your position, a position of trust, to satisfy your own prurient desires.

"I hope this sentence sends a message that society will not stand for these types of aberrations from the norm of what we expect from our educators and our clergy.

"In studying for the priesthood, I'm sure you became familiar with the many chapters and verses dealing with the punishment for the taking of another person's life. Starting with Cane and Able, and throughout the Old and New Testaments, the Holy Bible is very clear on the punishment to be prescribed. 'An eye for an eye and a tooth for a tooth'.

"Men much wiser than I wrote the gospels and the Bible, so how can I not abide by what these wise and holy men decided was the proper punishment for taking another's life?

   I hereby sentence you to be transferred to the penitentiary at Sing Sing, and, there to be executed after you have exhausted all your appeals. May God have mercy on your soul, because I certainly won't."

Confessions, Lies, and Secrets   *Stu Milisci*

CHAPTER 36

Death Row

Andrew Watson, convicted of murder in the first degree and sentenced to be executed, was handcuffed, taken from the courtroom, and processed. He then began the trip upstate to Sing Sing Prison where he would stay on Death Row until all his appeals had been exhausted, and then be electrocuted.

He couldn't afford to hire an attorney to set forth the appeal procedure, so he would languish on Death Row with little chance of an appeal or a pardon. A few weeks prior to Watson's conviction, on August 15th, Eddie Lee Mays had been executed in Sing Sing for killing a woman in a Manhattan bar during a robbery. As it turned out, he would be the last person to sit in "Old Sparky" in that prison.

Many people, including Benjamin Franklin and other signers of the Declaration of Independence had tried to have the death penalty abolished. In Salem Massachusetts, in 1692, nineteen men and women were led to the gallows after being convicted of being *witches*. Prior to the twentieth century, hangings without trials were commonplace in the South and the West. Throughout the twentieth century, many states abolished capital punishment for most capital offenses except those deemed to be the most serious.

The arguments for and against capital punishment continued for many decades. Proponents argued capital punishment was justified when aggravating circumstances made a murder so heinous death was the only reasonable punishment. They also felt capital punishment acted as a deterrent to future murders and those convicted of murder, who were incarcerated for life, had nothing to lose by killing while in prison.

Opponents felt capital punishment was unwarranted under any circumstances since it was cruel and unusual punishment and wasn't a deterrent to future murders.

In New York State, in 1965, legislation was enacted to limit the death penalty to murder in the first degree when the victim was a peace officer performing his or her official duties, when the convicted felon was serving a life sentence at the time the crime was committed, if the crime was committed when the prisoner was serving an indeterminate sentence of at least fifteen years to life, or if the defendant was in immediate flight from penal custody or confinement when the crime was committed.

Since Andrew Watson's crime didn't meet any of these new conditions, he had a temporary stay of execution, although he remained on death row. His future was limited to a lifetime of confinement where he would spend 23 hours a day in a six foot by ten foot cell where he would eat, sleep, and take care of his personal needs in plain view of other inmates and guards.

    He would be allowed out for one hour per day to exercise with other death row inmates in a small outdoor yard, which would be his only human contact while incarcerated. He was allowed one visit and three phone calls per week.

    Detective Musto and Louis Caruso visited occasionally, and all of Andy's calls were made to these two men who hadn't given up on getting an appeal. He would spend his time reading, praying, exercising, and trying to maintain his physical and mental health. It had been established many death row inmates went insane during years of solitary confinement and about one forth of them died of suicide or natural causes while waiting for their sentences to be carried out.

Confessions, Lies, and Secrets   *Stu Milisci*

CHAPTER 37

Call Me "PADRE"

Andy Watson had accepted the reality he would spend the rest of his life incarcerated on Death Row in Sing Sing Prison. He realized he didn't have the resources for an appeal and resigned himself to his fate as the Will of God. He knew he was innocent and that's what really mattered. He was at peace with himself and his maker.

  Child molesters and child murderers are among the least popular inmates in prison. Even convicted murderers have a certain sense of morality and code of conduct. Often, those convicted of crimes involving violence against children are killed in prison by other inmates, but Andy's fellow inmates on death row believed he was innocent. While most incarcerated prisoners will attest to their innocence no matter how guilty they are, Andy's case was different. The other inmates became familiar with the details of Andy's case and felt he wasn't given a fair trial and shouldn't have been convicted on the limited

Confessions, Lies, and Secrets   *Stu Milisci*

evidence against him. Andy wasn't harassed by the other inmates who genuinely liked him and had taken to calling him "Padre." He was well educated, unlike most of the other inmates, and started reading law books and helped some of the others prepare for appeals. He also counseled them on faith and some of the inmates made peace with their maker. This gave Andy more satisfaction than it gave the inmates. He had dedicated his life to preach the word of God and no one could stop him from doing that even while in prison.

CHAPTER 38

The Intervening Years

Father Rooney passed away a year after Andy started serving his sentence still believing in Andy's innocence. Judge Glass died the following year still believing in his guilt. ADA Harold Shapiro, catapulted by his conviction in the Watson trial, was elected District Attorney of Kings County where he served even longer than his predecessor. He recruited Detective Maurice Gold to his office where he became one of his lead and best investigators thanks, in no small part, to his training at the heels of Detective Mike Musto.

     Mike Musto remained a detective in the NYPD until 1985, when he was forced to retire since he had reached the mandatory age of 62. He became a legend and often traveled to other jurisdictions to help solve cases, which proved to be too difficult for the local police.

Confessions, Lies, and Secrets   *Stu Milisci*

Anna Ruiz remained with the Public Defenders' Office until she was appointed to a judgeship at the New York State Court of Appeals. She always felt a little guilty for not giving Andrew Watson the kind of defense she knew she was capable of providing. She was put at ease when his death sentence was commuted. It would be easier for her to live with the fact a possibly innocent man might spend the rest of his life in prison, than to see him put to death.

Steven's older brother, Louis, had attended Andy Watson's trial and was convinced of his innocence. He decided he would become a lawyer and do everything in his power to have his conviction overturned and have the guilty party bought to justice. After graduation from Boston College, he entered Fordham Law School, earned his law degree, passed the bar exam, and started practicing criminal defense law. He conferred often with Mike Musto, who also was convinced of Andrew Watson's innocence. Together they worked to find a basis for an appeal in the Andrew Watson case.

Mr. Savino was ordained a priest shortly after the end of the trial. He was sent to the Phillipines where he remained for three years doing missionary work. After another two years assigned to The Vatican, he returned to the United States where he, once again, was relegated to teaching at the same school where he had taught as a seminarian, Loyola Jesuit High School in Brooklyn, NY. He refrained from counseling the boys as he had done in the past or having any physical contact with any of the students since he realized certain people were still suspicious of his involvement in Steven Caruso's death.

CHAPTER 39

More About Mike

Mike Musto found himself at age sixty-two forced to retire from a job he had devoted his entire adult life to. He went from one day being the best and most sought after homicide detective in the country, to being unemployed with nothing, but time on his hands.

He had been so involved with his career he never had time to develop any hobbies. He didn't golf, fish, or hunt and wasn't about to start at this stage in his life. He never married and had no family. He realized early on being a cop's wife required a special type of woman. All too often he saw his married friends' marriages end in divorce because they missed too many weddings, birthdays, and holidays. They had little time with their families because they couldn't get time off from the responsibilities of the job. Often cops would have to work a second job to make ends meet if they had a family. For all of these reasons, Mike Musto had chose to remain single.

Confessions, Lies, and Secrets   *Stu Milisci*

When the Police Department finally gave in to the pressure from the police unions to allow their members to moonlight on a second job, many cops looked for outside employment to supplement their incomes. A law enforcement officer with four or more kids, which included lots of cops, was entitled to food stamps since their salaries were so low.

There were certain restrictions the department placed on outside employment. No one could work for any establishment that was licensed by the State Liquor Authority. This included bars, restaurants, catering halls, social clubs or any other establishments that sold liquor. The department wouldn't allow employment in an establishment licensed by the SLA because it felt it created a conflict of interest for the cop. Many illegal activities occurred in licensed premises. Under age drinking, selling of stolen articles, and the sale and use of illegal drugs were a few.

Before a cop was allowed to work another job, he had to notify the department, fill out an application and receive written permission to work. There were restrictions on when a cop could work, how many hours he could work and the type of work he was allowed to do.

Cops were often relegated to working long shifts in super markets, department stores and the like for next to minimum wage. Some cops, realizing they could make a lot more money in a bar or restaurant as a bouncer, decided to ignore the department's ban on these restrictions and took the chance of working in these places without permission.

One detective from Mike Musto's squad had taken a job in a local bar and was working there one night when there was an attempted robbery. The detective shot and killed the guy and was rewarded by losing his job. During the investigation into the incident, he said he had been a patron at the bar and didn't work there. Everyone at the bar backed up his story. When asked how long he had been at the bar and how much he had to drink, he said he had been there about an hour and had consumed two scotches. The department made him take a breathalyzer test which came back negative for any alcohol. He was charged with unauthorized off duty employment and lying during an official investigation and was fired from the Police Department.

    That detective had been on the job for twenty three years. He had been entitled to a half pay pension after his twentieth anniversary, but he had chosen to stay on the job. He was divorced and was paying alimony to his ex-wife and support for his two small children. He had met a woman who was a bar maid at the bar where he moonlighted. She had been married, but divorced from a wise guy who was serving a long prison sentence for his mob related activities. She had a child of her own. Unfortunately, she had become use to the "Wise Guy" mentality and way of life and most of her friends and acquaintances were shady characters. She borrowed money from two different loan sharks and was having a tough time paying the weekly three point "Vig."

    In addition to the other expenses the detective had, he was helping his new girlfriend pay off her loans to the loan sharks. He had fallen for her because at two o:clock in the morning, when you have lost your job, had no one to go

Confessions, Lies, and Secrets Stu Milisci

home to, you're in a dark bar, and you're judgment is clouded by alcohol, the flesh is weak.

One bright spring Sunday morning when the former detective was on his way to Staten Island for his weekly court approved visit with his children, the former detective pulled over on the Verrazano Bridge, got out of his car, walked to the bridge railing, climber over, and jumped into the clear waters below.

Mike Musto had seen and heard of many stories about cops burning out on the job and taking the coward's way out. The most common cause was fear of losing their hard earned pension because of some simple violation of department rules and procedures the Police Department would pursue, investigate, and punish.

This was the type of hypocrisy and administration Mike had grown to hate. He wouldn't miss this kind of crap at all.

Now he had to decide what to do with the rest of his life. He could have gotten a job as a civilian investigator for the Brooklyn DA's Office. In addition to detectives from the NYPD assigned to the DA's office, there were a number of retired detectives who were welcomed there as investigators after they retired. That would have meant working for his old associate, Harold Shapiro, who was currently the elected District Attorney for Kings County.

One of Mike's highest priorities was to have Andrew Watson's conviction overturned on appeal, and working for the man who had prosecuted the case and gotten a conviction didn't seem like a good place to start. DA Shapiro wasn't about to open a can of worms over an old case he had won.

Confessions, Lies, and Secrets   *Stu Milisci*

    Over lunch one day shortly after Mike retired, he and Louis Caruso were discussing Mike's possible career choices. Mike had met many characters during his long career in the police department and liked nothing better than to tell stories about the lighter and more personal side of police work.

    When Mike was a new detective he was partnered with a veteran named Harry "The Horse" Hendriks. Harry didn't get his nick name because he had an affinity for thoroughbred racing, but rather for the size of a certain part of his anatomy. Harry was what was known as a "ladies' man" and he had lots of woman friends throughout the years. His current girlfriend lived close to the station house and whenever Harry left the office for a court appearance or to interview a witness, he would stop by for a little afternoon delight.

    The holidays were coming and his girlfriend, knowing Harry was off on New Year's Eve, started busting his chops about being together and going to the city to celebrate with the millions of people who gathered in Times Square every year to watch the ball drop from a building at One Times Square Center. She also wanted to celebrate at The Roosevelt Hotel where it was a tradition for band leader Guy Lombardo and his Royal Canadians to bring in the New Year with a festive party.

    So Harry told his wife, who he always referred to as "The bride," he had to work New Year's Eve on a special detail. His tour would be from 6:00 p.m. until 2:00 a.m., which would allow him plenty of time to be with his girlfriend in the city. Harry left his home at about four in the afternoon and went directly to his girlfriend's apartment

Confessions, Lies, and Secrets   *Stu Milisci*

where he changed into a tuxedo he had rented the day before. Then it was off to the city to celebrate.

"The bride" was home alone and decided to stay up until midnight so she could watch the festivities on television. Just after midnight the broadcast went from Times Square to a live shot of Guy Lombardo at the Roosevelt Hotel. As the camera panned across the dance floor showing couples dressed in formal wear dancing, sure enough, "The bride' saw "The horse" dancing with a lovely blonde.

When Harry finally got home, he had some fast thinking and smooth talking to do. When confronted by his wife, he told her the Police Department had received information an anti administration group was going to protest at The Roosevelt Hotel during the live television broadcast and he had been assigned to work undercover at the ballroom to keep an eye on things and report any suspicious characters.

"The bride" didn't really believe him, but the story was almost credible so "The Horse" was allowed to stay in the stable. He no longer referred to his wife as, "The bride". His new pet name for her was, "That nagging bitch." He died of AIDS a few years later without ever getting a penny of his pension. Fortunately for his wife, Harry had more than twenty years of service in the police department and was covered by the "Death Gamble" which was a benefit which kicked in when an active member died while still employed and had more than twenty years on the job.

He was presumed to have taken a service retirement the day before he died, so "The nagging bitch" got Harry's pension. As unfaithful as he had been, he must have really loved her to make sure she was provided for in this way after he was gone.

After Mike finished telling Louis this story, and Louis stopped laughing, they got around to a more serious discussion.

Like Mike, Louis felt Andrew Watson was innocent and had been railroaded. He told Mike his heavy case load didn't allow him the time to dedicate to try to win an appeal. He also had a wife and two young sons who required a lot of his time and energy when he wasn't working. He named his first born Joseph after his father which was almost mandatory in Italian families. He named his younger son Steven for obvious reasons.

He was amazed how much Steven reminded Louis of his deceased brother and how much alike they looked. If you held a photo of each of them side by side at the same age, you couldn't tell them apart. This resemblance was a constant reminder to Louis of his own brother and a catalyst to continue to pursue his murderer.

Since Louis averaged sixty hour work weeks, it didn't leave him much time for family activities. He offered Mike a job at the law firm where he was an associate. They were a criminal defense firm and many of their cases involved attempts to get verdicts appealed. Mike would interview witnesses, secure depositions, gather evidence, and sit in on trials and appeals.

Mike wondered if he could jump over to the other side of the fence after trying for convictions for forty years, but realized justice was what really mattered. All too often he had seen ruthless young prosecutors bend the rules and railroad some poor defendant just to up their conviction rates. He also knew working for a criminal defense law firm would give him the time and necessary resources to work on Andew Watson's appeal.

    Mike decided to accept the offer and took the job.

CHAPTER 40

More About Louis

By the time Andrew Watson's trial began in the summer of 1963, Louis had completed his freshman year at Boston College. Since his parents chose not to attend the court trial, it was left to Louis to be present to represent the Caruso family. He was in court every day, and paid very close attention to the proceedings. He thought Father Watson was innocent and didn't think the prosecution could get a conviction based on the one piece of evidence found at the scene of the crime.

He also thought the young female defense attorney could have done a much better job in defending Father Watson. She didn't challenge any prospective jurors, didn't offer much in the way of cross examination, called only three witnesses for the defense, and had never asked for a change of venue. He did feel her closing argument planted enough reasonable doubt in the minds of the jurors to win

Confessions, Lies, and Secrets   *Stu Milisci*

an acquittal, but that was not to be.

Andrew Watson was convicted of murder in the first degree. The entire episode made Louis decide to become a lawyer with the hope of one day being able to get an appeal for Watson and have his verdict overturned.

Louis attended Fordham Law School after getting his B.A. degree from Boston College. He passed the bar exam and took a position as an associate attorney with a New York law firm which concentrated on representing clients in criminal cases.

He married a neighborhood girl and they had two sons. He bought a house in Brooklyn Heights which wasn't too far from the Red Hook neighborhood where he grew up, but they could have been on different planets because they were so different. He lived in a three story converted brownstone town house with twelve foot ceilings and thick mahogany moldings in every room. The law firm he worked for was on Court Street in Brooklyn and, on pleasant days, he would walk the twenty minutes it took him to go from his home to his office.

CHAPTER 41

More About Anna Ruiz

Anna Ruiz had gotten her wish and had been appointed a judge in The New York State Court of Appeals. She spent years honing her skills as a defense attorney working for the Legal Aid Society. She was so dedicated to her work and her causes she had very little time for a social life, dating, or marriage. Without the distractions and obligations of a husband and children, she plunged into her work with dedication and determination that bordered on the obsession. She was a true champion of civil rights and wrote many decisions and gave many speeches about the injustices of the criminal justice system and it's unfair treatment of minorities. She was an agnostic with little conscious.

  Anna Ruiz was extremely liberal in her views. She was pro abortion, anti capital punishment, and a staunch proponent of equal pay for equal work. Her notoriety as an outspoken supporter of the liberal agenda got the attention of many politicians. She was well known and respected, attractive, intelligent, and seen as a vote getter among women and minorities.

She campaigned for the Democratic candidate for Governor of New York, and, with her help, he was elected. As a reward for her help in getting him elected, he named her to the position of Attorney General of the State of New York with the promise, if he ever got elected to be president (which was his long term objective), he would appoint her to the Supreme Court as his first appointment to that prestigious institution. With her background and notoriety she'd have no trouble being confirmed by a liberal senate.

Anna had come a long way from those early days as a defense attorney. So far, all her hopes and dreams had been fulfilled, but she still had some misgivings about Andrew Watson's conviction for first degree murder. She knew she could have presented a much better defense and probably could have gotten an acquittal if she had truly wanted to. But she set her sights on helping get the governor into the White House and one day being appointed to The Supreme Court. This was a goal that far exceeded her expectations when she was a young attorney working for the Legal Aid Society.

CHAPTER 42

DNA

Through his work as a defense attorney, Louis Caruso met another young attorney from New York named Barry Scheck. In 1988, Barry Scheck, along with his partner, Peter Neufeld, became involved in studying and litigating issues concerning the use of forensic DNA testing. DNA was a new scientific discovery, which would become one of the most important innovations in forensic evidence.

DNA, or deoxyribonucleic acid, is the hereditary material in humans and almost all other organisms. It, like fingerprints, is unique to every individual with the exception of identical twins who share the same DNA. The introduction of DNA in criminal cases would serve not only to help get convictions for guilty suspects, but, perhaps more importantly, to exonerate defendants convicted of crimes they didn't commit.

In 1992, Barry Scheck and Peter Neufeld founded the Innocence Project, a New York based non-profit legal organization committed to exonerating wrongly convicted people through the use of DNA testing. They hoped it would reform the criminal justice system to prevent future injustice. Their work was mostly pro bono, and they had early success in reversing a number of wrongful convictions. Barry Scheck would earn worldwide notoriety when in 1995 he would be a part of the, "Dream Team" that obtained an acquittal for O.J. Simpson in a double homicide case involving the murder of his ex-wife, Nicole Brown Simpson, and her friend, Ronald Goldman.

They worked pro bono since most of their clients were members of poor minorities who were only convicted in the first place because they couldn't afford to hire a decent defense attorney.

CHAPTER 43

Getting An Appeal

Mike Musto learned a few things during his more than forty years as a cop. After Andrew Watson's conviction, Mike gathered all the evidence in the case and brought it to the Police Department's Property Clerk's Office with instructions to keep it there until such time as he could win an appeal to the case. He also had transcripts of all the testimony from the trial. He knew this would all be crucial in trying to get an appeal and to overturn Andrew Watson's conviction.

      During a conference at the offices of The Innocence Project, Barry Scheck, Peter Neufeld, Louis Caruso, and Mike Musto discussed a strategy they would use to try for an appeal. Mike told the others he had access to the evidence, which included the chair that had the skin and hair particles on one of its legs. They reviewed the testimony from the transcripts. There were several things they all agreed, taken together, were grounds for an appeal.

Confessions, Lies, and Secrets   *Stu Milisci*

The hair samples on the base of the chair leg didn't match Andrew Watson's hair. The attacker was almost certainly left handed and Watson was not. The prosecution had only one piece of circumstantial evidence, which could easily be challenged.

    They agreed, in light of all the adverse publicity at the time and the public's awareness of attempts by the Catholic Church to cover up allegations of sexual misconduct, the defense should have requested a change of venue in order to get an impartial jury. They also cited the fact neither side had challenged any of the jurors. The defense hadn't done much in the way of cross examination of prosecution witnesses and called only three defense witnesses of their own. The Legal Aid Society had assigned their least seasoned attorney, with no experience in capital cases, to defend the suspect in this highly publicized trial. They felt they could show Watson wasn't provided an adequate defense.

    They were certain they had enough material for an appeal, but decided, to bolster their case, they should do DNA testing on the substances on the chair leg. If that didn't match Watson's DNA it would prove he hadn't been the assailant.

    They had the DNA tested, took a sample from Andrew Watson and were able to determine there was no match to the substance on the leg of the chair, which was submitted as evidence in the original trial. They felt they were now ready to request an appeal.

CHAPTER 44

Damage Control

There wasn't a lot that happened in the criminal justice system in New York State that Anna Ruiz wasn't privy to. She had found out about the negative results of the DNA testing and felt sure the defense team would move for an appeal. She realized an appeal in this case and a reversal of the conviction would look bad for her and negatively affect her future plans. She asked for an audience with the governor to discuss their options.

"Well, your honor, I asked for this meeting to discuss an old case which may be coming up for appeal."

"Which case might that be, Anna?" the governor inquired.

"It was a murder case back in the 60's which I defended. A Catholic priest was convicted and sentenced to death. His sentence was later commuted to life in prison."

This seemed to peak the governor's interest and he asked Anna to have a seat. "And why do you feel this might be a problem?"

"Well, it was early in my career and public pressure was strong for a conviction. I didn't go out of my way to present a credible defense. If the conviction is overturned on appeal, it may have a negative impact on my future plans. I doubt I would be confirmed for the Supreme Court with an overturned conviction on my resume.

"The ADA who prosecuted the case was Harold Shapiro who is now the District Attorney in Kings County. I'm sure he wouldn't be happy with a reversal upon appeal either. He is well respected among district attorneys and US Attorneys across the nation and could be a positive force in your run for the White House."

"I know Shapiro well, and agree he could be useful in my run for the oval office. What do you suggest we do?"

Anna stood and faced the governor. "Perhaps if you granted the convicted felon a pardon and he were released from prison, they would forget about the appeal. The conviction would still stand, but he'd be a free man. By all accounts he has been an exemplary prisoner and certainly wouldn't be a threat to society."

"Anna, I don't see a problem here. I doubt anyone remembers the case. It happened so long ago. Since you're the Attorney General, why don't you set the wheels in motion?"

So Anna did all the necessary work to grant a pardon, which the governor granted and, for the first time in thirty years, Andy Watson was a free man.

CHAPTER 45

Free At Last

The life and world Andrew Watson returned to were a lot different than the ones he had left. He had been a priest and an educator. He was the headmaster of a Jesuit High School and the pastor of a parish. Although he had been pardoned, he was still a convicted felon. As a former priest, he was no longer bound by his vows, although he didn't need a vow of poverty to be dirt poor. At his age and with a felony conviction for murder on his record, he certainly couldn't teach anywhere, nor could he get any type of job.

The Innocence Project set up a fund, which allowed Watson to get a small apartment and provided him with the bare essentials. He was happy to finally be free and didn't mind living such a meager life. What he wanted most of all now was to be exonerated of the crime he had been convicted of and hadn't committed. He sat in on meetings with Mike and the attorneys to discuss their next moves.

Confessions, Lies, and Secrets   *Stu Milisci*

Andy told them although he was happy to be free, he wanted to pursue an appeal to be exonerated, have his conviction overturned, and restore his good name.

CHAPTER 46

Confessing a Confession

Mike Musto always felt Andrew Watson knew more about the circumstances of Steven Caruso's death than he told him at the time of the trial. He sensed Watson had been holding something back. Being a Catholic himself, Mike wondered if Watson had been told something in the confessional he was forbidden to share because of his priestly vows. Mike got together with Watson, one on one, and conducted an interview.

"Andy, back when you were arrested and I interviewed you, I felt there were things you knew, but you weren't telling me. While I respected the fact you were a priest at the time and there were certain things you were obligated not to divulge, I'd like to remind you that you are no longer a priest, you are no longer required to maintain the confidentiality of priest and penitent, and you have spent more than thirty years in prison.

Confessions, Lies, and Secrets　　　　　　　*Stu Milisci*

    The Catholic Church certainly didn't provide any assistance in your defense. In fact, they sold you out and made sure you were no longer a priest by the time the trial started. I admired the fact you were willing to be convicted, faced with the death penalty, and wound up being in jail for so long because you refused to compromise your ethics.
    But that was then and this is now. I'm sure one of your highest priorities is having your conviction thrown out and proving you are innocent. Whoever committed this murder was willing to see you die in the electric chair, so you certainly have no allegiance to whomever that may be. If there is anything that will help us win an appeal for you, now would be a good time to let me know."
    Watson felt a great sense of relief as Mike spoke. For years he struggled with the decision to come forward and divulge what Steven had confessed. Mike had given him an opportunity to do just that.
    "Mike, you're an exceptional judge of character. You are correct. There were things I knew which I wasn't able to divulge. I wrestled with this for a long time while I was in prison. My stubborn adherence to the laws of a church which refused to believe in me after serving them loyally for so many years, and sold me out so easily, began to make less and less sense to me with the passage of years.
    "Steven Caruso came to me for confession full of guilt. He told me a story of a sexual assault by a member of the faculty at the school. He did not name his assailant. I implored him to report this incident to the police. I gave him absolution and told him to relieve himself of any guilt

he felt. I believe he confronted his assailant, threatened to go to the police and was murdered. The murderer had to be someone with access to the cafeteria, and Steven had told me in confession his attacker was a member of the faculty."

"Father do you have any suspicions as to who may have done this?"

Watson turned toward Musto with a quizzical look on his face. "Slip of the tongue, Mike? No one has addressed me as that for many years. Here you are, on the one hand trying to convince me to disregard my previous vows as a priest, and on the other hand, you address me as 'Father'."

Musto raised his hands in frustration, "Come on, Andy. I'm trying to help you here."

"I know you are Mike. I'm very grateful for all the work you've done to give me back my freedom and, hopefully, my good name.

"I've always suspected Mr. Savino. He was Steven's homeroom teacher and adviser. He had the most access to him. I hate to accuse anyone of something without proof, but if you're asking for an opinion based on my recollections, I'd have to go with Mr. Savino.

"I knew him when he was a student at the school. I taught him and got to know him pretty well. Later, after he finished seminarian school, he returned to Loyola as a teaching scholastic while I was headmaster, and I got to know him even better. He always seemed a little odd to me both as a student and as a teacher."

Confessions, Lies, and Secrets *Stu Milisci*

CHAPTER 47

The Appeal

The results of the DNA testing done on the skin and hair particles that were on the leg of the folding chair, found at the crime scene, proved not to be a match to Andrew Watson. Based on these new developments, the defense team felt there were two things they had to do. The first was to have Watson's conviction thrown out. The second was to try to find out who's DNA it was and have a trial convened against this new suspect.

The DNA result would have a twofold purpose. It would exonerate an innocent man who had spent more than thirty years in prison, and, hopefully, convict a guilty person who stood by and allowed it to happen.

Their first goal turned out to be a lot easier than their second. They presented this new evidence to a sitting judge who reviewed it and decided to have a court hearing to overturn the conviction of Andrew Watson. The hearing was held, the evidence presented, and the conviction was overturned.

For the first time in over thirty years, Andrew Watson was not only a free man, but he was also an innocent man.

Now all that was left to do for the defense team was to identify the real murderer, see him brought to trial, convicted, and sentenced.

CHAPTER 48

Making Their Case

After the euphoria and celebration of the conviction being overturned wore off, Watson and the defense team came together to decide their strategy. Barry Scheck and Peter Neufeld listened as each of the three other members present at the original trial spoke of their reasons to suspect James Savino as being Steven Caruso's murderer.

Steven's brother, Louis Caruso, was the first to speak.

"I never had James Savino as a teacher since he came to the school when I was in my second year and he taught freshmen. He did seem to go out of his way to befriend me. At the time, I didn't feel his interest in me was unusual since we were both Italian and I was a good athlete trying to get into a decent college. He had a keen interest in sports. He was young and seemed to be deeply interested in the growth and accomplishments of the boys at the school.

Confessions, Lies, and Secrets *Stu Milisci*

"Steven started Loyola right after I graduated. He had James Savino as a home room teacher and for Latin and Theology. Steven told me about Mr. Savino's interest in him and his guidance. I remember thinking it may have been a little over the top. Savino made him the class beetle, went to all the football games, most of the track meets and convinced Steven to run for class president.

"Steven never mentioned he had any doubts or misgivings about the attention he got from Mr. Savino, so I put my suspicions aside and never said anything to Steven about them.

"Before Steven's death, Mr. Savino talked to our parents regularly about Steven's progress and his hopes and aspirations for Steven's future. After Steven was murdered and before the trial began, Mr. Savino didn't contact my parents at all to offer his condolences or try to give them any comfort. As far as I know, he had no contact with them at all after Steven's death.

"This seemed to be strange behavior from a man who had taken such an interest in my brother and who was intent on becoming a priest. I expected a lot more from him."

Andrew Watson was the next to speak.

"At the time of Steven's murder, I had no more reason to suspect James Savino than any other member of the faculty. Steven told me during confession he had an unwanted sexual incident with an unnamed teacher at the school. That could have been any one of almost twenty people. The police had more suspects than that since they didn't know it was a teacher who committed this crime.

Anyone who resided at the rectory could have gotten into my unlocked room and removed the chain and crucifix, from the night table next to my bed while I slept. I wasn't aware of any special attention Mr. Savino was giving to Steven. We had more than six hundred students and twenty or so teachers at the time and it would have been impossible for me to track the daily interactions of all of them.

I only became aware of issues when they became problems and I was called upon to try to solve them. Had I known about Mr. Savino's special interest at the time, I would have considered it a little excessive and unusual. Since Louis had done so well and gotten a scholarship to Boston College, and his parents knew how Mr. Savino had helped that to happen, I'm sure they welcomed his interest in Steven hoping he too would get a scholarship."

The former detective was the next to speak. "I always believed Andy to be innocent. I realized the only evidence in the case was the chain and crucifix. I felt that could easily have been planted at the crime scene and never felt Andy should have been indicted or arrested based solely on that evidence. I also knew there was a lot of pressure from different directions for a quick arrest and conviction.

"I felt the folding chair with the human tissue at the foot of one of the legs was at least as important a piece of evidence as the crucifix. Unfortunately, DNA didn't exist at the time. I tried to establish by personal observation of who the tissue may have come from. The day after the crime, we assembled all the people who were present at the rectory the night of the crime and tried to identify anyone who looked like they had been hit in the head with a chair. There was no one who had any apparent injury to his head, but Mr. Savino had a full head of curly dark brown hair and could have easily combed his hair in a way that would have covered an injury to his scalp. He was also one of only three possible suspects who was left handed and I felt sure, based on Steven's defensive wound to his right arm, his assailant was left handed. These facts definitely made me want to look at Mr. Savino more closely, but I wasn't allowed to.

"My instincts and experience as a detective made me feel strongly Savino looked good as a suspect, but everyone was in such a rush to judgment. I wasn't allowed to try to make a case against him. I was ordered to arrest Father Watson."

Feeling they were productive, the group decided to meet again the following day to plan a strategy.

CHAPTER 49

Getting a DNA Sample

Still riding high from the successful meeting the day before, the group convened the next day with a new found energy. They agreed they had to get a DNA sample from Savino and match it to the sample on the chair leg. If the sample matched, they'd move for an arrest and indictment against him. Mike was no longer a cop and getting a warrant for a DNA sample would be a difficult thing to do. Since the Attorney General of the state and the Kings County District Attorney had been involved in the original trial, most judges wouldn't want to touch a warrant with a ten foot pole.

They decided they would have to come up with a plan to get a DNA sample from Savino on their own. They would also have to document that the sample came from him if a match were made, if they expected it to have any value as evidence in court.

Confessions, Lies, and Secrets   Stu Milisci

After many hours of brain storming and rejecting several plans, Andy came up with an idea.

"What if I were to call Father Savino and ask him to join me for lunch one afternoon? I'm sure this would raise some suspicion on his part, but it might be more suspicious if he refused to meet with me. It might look like he had something to hide. I can tell him, since he's the only priest that is still assigned to Loyola who was there when Steven got murdered, I'd like to meet with him and discuss any feelings he might have about who might have committed this crime so many years ago. Possibly he heard things during or after the trial."

Mike looked at Andy with an astonished expression. "You missed your calling, Andy. You woulda made a better detective than me. We can have you wear a wire to record the conversation and we can set up video surveillance. If we can get a cup or utensil he used, have video of it to prove it came from him, and then have it tested for DNA, we can establish chain of evidence, which would be proof positive any DNA recovered from the object came from Savino."

"I like it. I like it a lot."

CHAPTER 50

The Sting

"Hello, This is Andy Watson and I'm calling to speak to Father Savino if he's available."

The phone at the rectory was answered by a switchboard operator who had been doing the same job since Andy Watson was headmaster of the school. She was aware Andy's conviction had been thrown out.

"Oh yes, of course. Congratulations on your successful appeal. Please hold the line and I'll connect you in a moment."

Andy could hear another phone ringing on the line and he gave the team a thumbs up. After a few rings, Savino came on the line.

"Andy, so glad things went your way. I'm so happy you've finally been vindicated."

"Thank you, Father."

Confessions, Lies, and Secrets   *Stu Milisci*

"Andy, since I can no longer address you as Father, please call me Jim. I could never come close to being the priest you were. I feel uncomfortable hearing you call me Father."

"That's very nice of you, Jim. Your kind words warm my heart."

"So what can I do for you, Andy? You want a job at the school?"

"I doubt you're serious, but thanks for the offer. My teaching days are long over."

Savino continued with a more serious tone. "I realize you couldn't take a position at the school, but I remember what a great teacher and headmaster you were. You did so much for me when I was a student and, then again, later when I was a teaching scholastic. If it weren't for you, I would never have been a priest."

"Jim, I'm working with a team of attorneys who are trying to find justice for Steven Caruso. Since my conviction was overturned, it's apparent the guilty party is still out there. He may well be dead after so many years, but it's necessary to find out who did this horrible thing to get justice for Steven and his family. I thought we might meet for lunch one day and share our thoughts about what we recall about the incident."

Father Savino realized if he refused to meet with Andy, it would seem suspicious. He hadn't heard anything about how Andy Watson had been exonerated by the use of DNA evidence. In fact, he had never heard anything about DNA evidence and had no clue what it was.

"Andy, I'd love to see you. I can have someone take my afternoon classes tomorrow, which will free me up for the rest of the day. Do you remember that A&W fast food stand on Nostrand Avenue? It's not too far from the school and I've never lost my love of those root beer floats. I can meet you there at 12:30 if that's good for you."

"Jim, that would be great. Thanks so much for agreeing to meet with me."

Savino responded," Andy, Steven Caruso was in my class at the time of his death. He was a brilliant young man with a promising future. I certainly want to help in any way I can to bring his murderer to justice."

"Thank you, Jim. I'll see you tomorrow."

Confessions, Lies, and Secrets *Stu Milisci*

CHAPTER 51

Setting The Stage

Now the defense team had to come up with a plan that would allow them to gather some DNA from Savino. They realized the two men having lunch would be a perfect opportunity to get a DNA sample from Savino.

    They needed the cooperation of the manager of the restaurant to set the plan in motion. Mike had been a detective for so long he knew just about everyone who had a business within the boundaries of the 71st precinct. Mike paid the manager of the A&W restaurant a visit on the morning of the meeting between Andy and Savino. While he didn't tell the manager he was still an active detective, he also didn't tell him he had retired. He asked the manager's permission to have a female investigator from their office dress as a waitress and pretend to work there. He said it was part of an important investigation. The manager was a bit of a police buff and welcomed the opportunity of being part of a case.

Confessions, Lies, and Secrets Stu Milisci

With that part of the plan in place, Mike returned to the office. He chose a young female investigator named Genna Gordon who had majored in theater at Michigan State University and come to New York after college to follow her dream of becoming a Broadway star like so many other aspiring actresses. She had actually worked as a waitress to support herself while waiting for her acting career to take off. After a few years, she gave up acting and waitressing and joined the Innocence Project. Since she had done some acting while in school, she was a natural for surveillance work and role playing in sting operations. She looked like a waitress because she had been one and Mike explained what her role would be. She had worked other cases with Mike and was delighted to be part of this sting.

Barry Scheck and Peter Neufeld would arrive at the restaurant about half an hour before Andy and Savino got there. They would order some food and sit at a table. Peter would have a camera in his briefcase, which he would position in a way to get a good view of Andy and Savino. He would video record the entire meeting so it could be presented in court. They had to convince a jury the DNA taken from anything in the restaurant had come from Savino.

Andy was fitted with a recording device so there would be audio to go with the video.

Mike would be outside the restaurant in a van monitoring the entire proceedings.

Genna Gordon arrived at the restaurant at 10:00 a.m.. She reported to the manager, was given a uniform and introduced to the rest of the staff as a new waitress. Peter and Barry Scheck got there at noon, picked out a table which would give them a good view of Andy and Savino, ordered lunch and waited for Andy to arrive. Andy got there about twenty minutes later. Genna directed Andy to a table Peter Neufeld had selected, which had the best position for filming. It was important for Andy to arrive before Savino so he could sit at a table which allowed for a good camera angle. All this took place without arousing any suspicion among the employees.

James Savino arrived at precisely 12:30 p.m.. After greeting each other, Savino took a seat opposite Watson and ordered a cheeseburger, French fries, and a root beer float. His position was perfect for filming the entire meeting.

After some conversation, and a few bites from the cheeseburger, a couple of French fries, and a few sips from the root beer float, Andy knocked over Savino's cup. It appeared to be accidental. The waitress/investigator came to the table cleaned up the spill, took the overturned cup and gave Savino another float. She immediately left the restaurant and went over to the surveillance van where she gave the cup to Mike.

Andy and Savino finished their meals, their conversation, and their meeting. They shook hands, promised to meet again soon and left. Peter and Barry were the last to leave.

Once they all convened at the van, Mike placed the cup in an evidence envelope which he marked identifying what it was, where and when it had been obtained, and who had drunk from it. Its evidentiary value would be valid in any court of law.

Confessions, Lies, and Secrets   *Stu Milisci*

CHAPTER 52

A Conversation

The defense team returned to its offices and was pleased with the results of its sting operation. Everyone played their roles well and were sure Savino had no clue he was being recorded. They reviewed the audio and video several times. Savino hadn't said anything incriminating, but they had the cup he had drunk from and hoped to get a DNA sample from it.

Barry Scheck and Peter Neufeld were anxious to get the cup tested for DNA and left for the lab. Mike and Andy had the whole afternoon left without much to do.

"Andy, you were great under pressure with Savino. I'd like to buy you a beer if you have the time."

Andy responded eagerly, "I haven't sat at a bar and had a beer in a very long time and there's no one I'd rather have that beer with than you. When I got out of active duty,

Confessions, Lies, and Secrets   *Stu Milisci*

I was working full time and going to school at night, so I didn't have much free time to hang out in bars with my buddies. As a priest, one didn't want to be seen in a bar. As for the last thirty years, well we won't even get into that."

The two men left for a local bar where Mike was well known for an afternoon of drinking and conversation. One of the few luxuries Mike allowed himself while he was on the job was to stop by this bar with a few members of his squad after a particularly hectic day and unwind with a couple of beers.

"Andy, you were a priest for quite a while many years ago. A lot of things have changed since that time. Do you have any reason to think Savino was homosexual?"

"No, I don't."

"People's attitudes toward homosexuals have evolved. Today, homosexuals are accepted as a mainstream part of society. Back in the old days, they were ostracized, looked down upon, assaulted, and disgraced. Many of them feared losing their jobs if they were discovered. If a man didn't get married or date often, he was looked upon with suspicion. Many actors and other high profile persons who were homosexuals married to make it seem they were straight. People lived their entire lives hiding who they really were, in fear they wouldn't be accepted by mainstream society. Men married and had children, but that didn't change the fact they were homosexuals.

"The priesthood was the only profession or calling where a man certainly wasn't expected to get married or show any sexual interest in women. I think some homosexual men chose to become priests to hide their homosexuality."

"Mike, what you say makes sense. The Catholic Church never would admit to harboring homosexuals since they considered it sinful. There were certainly priests I knew whom I suspected were homosexuals. I never saw any overt acts committed that would prove it, but if a man entered the priesthood to hide his homosexuality, I doubt he would engage in any kind of conduct that would cause further suspicion.

I imagine they had a difficult time trying to be accepted in the environment of the Catholic Church knowing the church viewed homosexuality as a sin. Many of them, confronted with this dilemma, eventually left the church. One young priest who taught at Loyola while I was there committed suicide. I remember thinking at the time he was a homosexual and couldn't reconcile that with him being a Catholic priest. Then, all of a sudden, all of these allegations of sexual abuse by priests started to crop up and the public couldn't help but take notice and become suspicious of many of the clergy. It's like if a cop gets caught doing something wrong, then all cops are thought of as being corrupt."

"You don't have any reason to suspect Savino could be a homosexual?"

"I never saw any behavior on his part to suggest that, but you have to realize there is a difference between a homosexual and a pedophile. Homosexuals don't sexually attack children; pedophiles, or some pedophiles, do. Not all homosexuals are pedophiles and not all pedophiles are homosexuals."

Confessions, Lies, and Secrets   Stu Milisci

"Did Savino ever do or say anything to make you think he could have been a pedophile?"

"At the time of Steven's murder, I hadn't noticed anything in Savino's behavior to suggest he could have been a pedophile. Looking back, he seemed to be spending a lot of time with Steven Caruso. Maybe this should have raised a red flag, but I missed it at the time."

"Don't beat yourself up over it Andy. There were a lot of other people who were closer to Steven who didn't sense there was anything wrong. Hindsight can be twenty-twenty sometimes. I had a bad feeling about the guy the first time I met him. There were a lot of things that pointed to him as being Steven's killer."

"Let's hope we get a hit with the DNA so we can finally get Steven the justice he deserves."

"You ready to leave? I can give you a lift back to your apartment."

"Yeah Mike. Maybe we should go. I'm starting to get a buzz from these beers."

CHAPTER 53

DNA Results

Three days after the sting operation at the A&W restaurant, the defense team gathered at the offices of the Innocence Project to learn the results of the DNA testing. They all hoped for a positive match showing the DNA taken from the cup Savino drank from was identical to the DNA taken from the tissues on the leg of the chair recovered at the crime scene. In most criminal cases, a positive match of DNA results in an automatic conviction. DNA had proven Watson's innocence and now they hoped it would also prove Savino's guilt.

    The results came in from the lab and everyone listened attentively as Barry Scheck read the report. Apparently the lab wasn't able to recover enough DNA from the cup to match unequivocally with the DNA from the chair leg. While it didn't rule out Savino as a match, it also could have been a match to 77,000,000 other people.

This certainly wasn't something they could present to the court as proof of Savino's guilt.

They needed a new plan. They discussed the possibility of trying to get another DNA sample from Savino. They agreed a second attempt would raise too much suspicion on his part.

Mike Musto suggested he call Savino in for an interview and see if he could trick him into making some incriminating statements or, perhaps, even a confession. He had done such interrogations many times during his police career. Police officers were not mandated to tell the truth during these interrogations and Mike was very skilled at skirting the truth to get the kind of results which would lead to a conviction.

Mike spoke to Savino and told him he represented a group of lawyers who were looking into the case of Steven Caruso's murder. He wanted to interview him since he was one of the few witnesses at the time of the crime, who was still alive. He told Savino they had no new suspects, but they were looking over the old court transcripts and the evidence to see if something important had been missed in the rush to judgment to convict Andrew Watson. Savino, again not wishing to raise any suspicion, agreed to meet with Mike at the Innocence Project offices the next day.

CHAPTER 54

On The Hot Seat

"Father Savino, thank you for coming in. I'm sure you want justice for Steven as much as anyone since you had become so close to him while he was a student at your school."

"Of course, Detective. I'll do any thing I can to help."

Father Savino didn't know that Mike Musto was no longer an active detective in the NYPD. Mike said nothing to suggest he still was.

"Father, are you familiar with DNA evidence?"

"I've read a little about it. I think it's a little like fingerprints and no two people share the same DNA."

"With the exception of identical twins. Identical twins share the same DNA. Father, do you have an identical twin?"

"No. I'm an only child. My parents are both deceased. My father was also an only child. My mother had an older sister, my Aunt Maria, who was a spinster and she also passed away several years ago. As far as I know, I have no other living relatives. This makes my vocation as a teacher and a priest more fulfilling as I have no family to fill the void of being alone and I can devote all of my time and energy to my priestly duties."

"DNA can be gotten from skin and scalp samples, from bodily fluids and even from utensils someone may have used," the former detective explained.

"That's very interesting. I didn't know that," Savino responded.

"Do you remember having lunch with Andrew Watson the other day?"

"Yes. I believe it was Monday. We ate at the A&W restaurant on Nostrand Avenue."

"We recorded that luncheon on video tape. Why don't you sit back and view it while I play it for you."

So Mike played the tape while Father Savino watched. At the time it had happened, Savino had no reason to suspect Watson had knocked over his drink other than by accident, but while watching the tape, it was obvious it was a deliberate act. He saw the waitress come over to their table, clean up the spill and take the cup.

At this point, Mike stopped the tape. He pressed the intercom and asked to have Genna Gordon come into the interview room. A few minutes later, Genna came in and Savino recognized her as the same girl who had been the waitress at the restaurant who had served him and Andy. She was a long legged, blue eyed brunette with curves in all the right places. She had the kind of looks even a priest wouldn't soon forget. Savino realized he had been had. He thought Peter Neufeld looked familiar when he entered the office but he couldn't place him. Now he realized he was the same man he saw sitting a few tables away from him and Andy in the restaurant with a briefcase placed on top of his table pointing directly at him. He now knew the entire episode at the restaurant had been a deliberate set up.

"Genna, say hello to Father Savino."

"Hello, Father Savino."

Mike thanked Genna and told her she could leave. "We took that cup from the restaurant and had it tested for DNA. Then we matched it to DNA from the chair Steven struck you with the night you murdered him. It was an exact match. (This was a lie, but it fell within the parameters of what was legal during the interrogation of a suspect.) We now know for sure you murdered Steven Caruso. You can choose to go to court, have a trial and protest your innocence. A trial will surly bring out all the other despicable behavior you engaged in if you choose to go that route. Or you can choose to make a confession only to the murder and save yourself from the other ugly acts you committed. We know you sexually assaulted Steven Caruso on the night of the Class Social after leaving the A&W Restaurant. He confessed that to Father Watson who was bound not to reveal it at the time since he was a priest. Now Andy is no longer a priest and is no longer forbidden to reveal what Steven told him in the confessional. He will testify at trial to the revelations made to him during Steven's confession. Again, the former detective made statements that weren't necessarily true. Savino had no way to know if Steven had gone to confession or what he confessed had he gone. Mike suggested Steven had named Savino as his attacker in the confessional booth.

"You may leave here right now, get a lawyer and wait to be indicted, or you can sign a confession and have it done with. I can't promise you any leniency upon sentencing. Either way you'll spend the rest of your life in prison, but prison can be a very ugly place for pedophiles and child molesters."

Savino knew he was caught, but he wanted to explain and try to justify what he had done. As he began to weep, he said plaintively, "Detective, you don't understand. I never meant to hurt Steven. I loved Steven. I only did things that would help him to live up to his potential. I encouraged him to get involved in sports, study hard and run for class president. I was helping him to design a brilliant future. I never forced him to have sex with me. There was only one time and I wanted to show him how much I loved him. When he threatened to go to the police, I saw that as him rejecting me, and I couldn't accept that after all I had done for him. I'm sorry for what I did and, in a way, I'm glad it's finally come out."

Savino wrote out a full confession admitting he had stabbed Steven Caruso to death in the school cafeteria. There was nothing mentioned about the sexual assault that took place prior to the murder. As part of a guilty plea, it was promised that Savino would only be charged with the murder and not the sexual assault. This might make things a little less dangerous for him in prison. If it became known in prison he was a homosexual and a child molesting pedophile, there's no telling what would happen to him at the hands of the other inmates.

The hand written confession was signed by Savino, witnessed by two employees of the law firm, and notarized by Peter Neufeld. It could now be presented in court as a legal document.

After the confession was completed, Savino was allowed to leave. He was told to get his affairs in order, hire an attorney, not leave town, and expect to hear from the DA's office very soon.

Confessions, Lies, and Secrets   *Stu Milisci*

CHAPTER 55

The DA's Case

Mike Musto called the Brooklyn District Attorney's Office and spoke to DA Shapiro. He gave a brief account of what happened with Savino and requested, and was granted, a meeting the following day.

"So, Mike, I can see you've been keeping yourself busy since your retirement. First you got Watson's conviction overturned and now you're trying for a conviction with another defendant."

"Harold, I'm kinda glad in a way I was forced out of the police department. It gave me time to work on Andrew Watson's appeal, have his conviction overturned, and bring the right man to justice."

"Mike, I'm glad Watson was exonerated. At the time of his arrest and trial it seemed obvious to everyone he was guilty. That was before DNA and other forensic science was available. On the basis of what evidence we had then, I felt we had a good case against Watson and proceeded on that basis. My job was to prosecute defendants based on the evidence we had available and try to get a conviction. That's exactly what I did in this case."

Musto, raising his voice, replied, "And I made my feelings about his innocence known to you in no uncertain terms. You ordered me to make the arrest and I complied. That was the first and only time in my entire career I arrested someone for a crime who I thought was innocent. I've never really forgiven you for forcing me into violating my integrity as a detective. I've never planted evidence on a suspect, committed perjury on the stand, or done anything else I considered unethical to get a conviction. I still have one of the highest conviction rates in the department."

"Mike, the system isn't perfect, but it's the best we've been able to come up with. We do the best we can with what we have available. Do some bad guys get cut loose because of some technical glitch that was overlooked during trial? Of course they do. As hard as we try, on very few occasions some poor innocent guy gets convicted of a crime he didn't commit. That's why we have an appeal system. In Watson's case, that worked too. Although granted it took a lot longer than it should have."

"Harold, don't talk to me about glitches. You knew the case against Watson stunk from the beginning. He never should have been arrested,or tried or convicted based on the one piece of evidence we had available at the time. His conviction helped put you in the chair you now occupy. It put Anna Ruiz on the fast track to becoming the highest ranking law enforcement officer in the state.

"I've never seen such a feeble defense presented in all my years as a detective. That case never should have been tried in Kings County. There was too much adverse publicity prior to the trial for Watson to have a chance at an acquittal. There should have been a change of venue. Not one juror was challenged by either side. The judge was a one sided, bible quoting, senile old man, and the defense called, what was it, three witnesses!"

"Mike, I had no control over what other people did in this case. I did my job and got a conviction. Which is what I'm supposed to do. Watson's exoneration caused me some discomfort."

"Not nearly as much DISCOMFORT as Andrew Watson had for more then thirty years on death row."

"Mike arguing like this is getting us nowhere. Can we discuss the reason for this meeting today?"

"You're right, Harold. 'Water under the bridge'."

"As you can see, I have with me a signed, witnessed, and notarized confession written by James Savino. He admits to murdering Steven Caruso. As part of an agreement with him, he'll plead guilty to that murder, so long as there are no charges involving sexual abuse. If you choose to, you can also charge him with sexual abuse. Watson is willing to testify to the fact Steven confessed to him he had been sexually abused by one of the teachers at the school. If you just go with the murder charge, there will be no need for a long drawn out trial. The confession should lead to an easy conviction. It would be difficult to get a conviction for a crime committed more then thirty years ago if we go to trial. Many witnesses are dead and the remaining ones might have difficulty with their

Confessions, Lies, and Secrets   *Stu Milisci*

recollections of what happened so many years ago. I lied to Savino about the DNA. It would be useless to us in a trial. Based on just his confession, it might be a tough case to prosecute if it goes to trial."

    "I agree with you completely, Mike. If a defense attorney could get the confession thrown out, which I'm sure he'd try to do, we'd really not have much of a case.

    "I'll have your old partner, Murice Gold, make the arrest. We'll agree to the deal on the table, have Savino plead guilty upon arraignment and finally put this case in the archives."

CHAPTER 56

A New Trial

The DA got together with Savino and his defense attorney and they hammered out a deal by which Savino would plead guilty to the crime of murder and not be charged with any other crimes. The sentence would have been the same even if other charges were lodged against him. The DA was satisfied he'd have a conviction which would put Savino away for the rest of his life and not have to take the chance of losing the case if it went to trial.

    Savino pled guilty at arraignment and was remanded to Rikers Island while a probation report was prepared. A sentencing date was set for two weeks after the arraignment at which time James Savino was sentenced to be executed. This sentence actually meant life in prison without parole since no one had been executed in New York for more than thirty years. He would serve his sentence on death row in Sing Sing Prison where Andrew Watson had been incarcerated for more than thirty years.

Confessions, Lies, and Secrets   *Stu Milisci*

      Savino was transported upstate to the prison and upon his arrival he was given his bedding, clothing, and toiletry articles. He was also given a form to fill out. He left many of the captions blank including relatives (since he had none) and who to notify in case of serious illness or death (for the same reason). He was escorted to a six foot by ten foot cell in a cell block on death row which would become his home for the rest of his life.

CHAPTER 57

Honor Among Thieves

Honor among thieves. Can there really be such a thing? Can convicted criminals actually have a code of moral behavior they believe in and live by? Everyone can decide for himself. Unless you've spent time in a prison, or had the opportunity to interview prisoners about their experiences over an extended period of time, it's difficult to answer that question.

Prisoners have their own hierarchy of inmates. For the most part, people imprisoned for white-collar crimes or property crimes not involving any violence are jailed in low security prisons away from the more violent inmates. Prisoners who have committed the more violent crimes are housed in more secure institutions. Murderers are usually the most respected and feared inmates in a prison. Those serving life sentences have little to lose by trying to dominate the rest of the population while incarcerated. Sex offenders, especially those whose victims included children, are the most hated and harassed. They are often assaulted and sometimes killed by fellow inmates.

While James Savino had been the recipient of a huge break by being charged only with murder, everyone at Sing Sing knew the details of Steven Caruso's death. Guards and prisoners alike knew Savino had also sexually assaulted Steven before murdering him.

Many of the death row inmates who were there when Andrew Watson was first imprisoned had died, but some were still alive. New inmates quickly learned of the innocent man in their midst and grew to respect him. Guards came and went, but they too sensed Watson was innocent and respected him almost as much as the inmates did.

It was clear to Savino as soon as he arrived at the prison that everyone knew the details of his sexual assault and murder of a young boy. News travels fast in most prisons. They knew he had allowed a decent and innocent man to rot on death row for over thirty years. They also knew he had sexually assaulted a young boy and then murdered him. They knew he had planted evidence, which got Watson convicted of a crime Savino had committed.

Realizing his life on death row was in serious jeopardy, Savino remained in his cell his first two days to avoid contact with any of the other inmates. He felt certain they would impose their own prison justice on him at the earliest possible opportunity.

CHAPTER 58

Justice

Just before lights out in all prisons, a count is made in all the cells to account for the inmates. If the count is short, it usually means a prisoner has tried to escape or has been killed.

On the third night of his incarceration, James Savino was missing from his cell during this nightly ritual. It was almost certain he hadn't tried to escape. A search was immediately conducted. After several minutes Savino's naked body was found hanging from an overhead pipe in the shower room. A makeshift noose had been fashioned from braided bed sheets and placed around his neck. His genitals had been removed and placed in his mouth. It was unable to be established if his body had been mutilated before or after the hanging.

While suicides are quite common in prisons, there was no doubt this was not a suicide.

Confessions, Lies, and Secrets   *Stu Milisci*

    Potter's Field located on Hart Island is a cemetery maintained by The Department of Corrections. It's a short bus ride from Rikers Island. It's a public burial place for paupers, unknown persons, and criminals.

    The guards took down Savino's body, placed it in a pine box, transported it to Potter's Field and buried it. Since Savino had not listed any family members on the forms he filled out three days prior to his death, there were no notifications to be made or any dispute as to where he would be buried.

    Reports by the guards listed the cause of death as suicide with no mention about the mutilation of Savino's body.

EPILOGUE

May 8, 1952

One of the requirements for seniors at Loyola Prep prior to graduation was to attend the Gonzaga Retreat House. The beautiful grounds are maintained by the Society of Jesus in upstate Monroe, New York.

About a month before graduation, the senior class spends five days meditating, praying, and cleansing their spirits and their souls. Their daily routine starts with morning prayers at 6:30 a.m., followed by daily mass, outdoor stations of the cross, and classes focused on trying to encourage some of the boys to consider the priesthood as a vocation.

The retreat facility had its own priests permanently assigned to conduct the retreat, but priests from the school accompanied the boys upstate and were an integral part of the program. The faculty knew the students since they were freshmen and felt if any of them needed special guidance or counseling while on retreat, they would be the ones who were best qualified to give it.

James Savino took part in this annual ritual in his final year as a student at Loyola Prep. His class adviser, Father Andrew Watson, had accompanied the boys as was customary. The housing consisted of a dormitory style four-story building. Each story had twenty rooms, and each room was shared by two boys. Each floor also had a private room at the end of the hallway nearest the staircase, where a priest would sleep. From this vantage point, he would be able to keep an eye on the boys assigned to that floor.

On the last night of the retreat, Father Watson was walking through the hallway of the floor he was assigned to monitor. Just after the lights were turned off in all the boys' rooms, he wanted to make sure everything was in order before he went to bed. As he passed by one of the rooms, he heard what sounded like a fight taking place inside. He entered the room to find James Savino and his roommate in the middle of a scuffle. When Father Watson demanded an explanation, James's roommate told the priest James had wanted to have sex with him and when he refused, they started fighting. James's roommate was told to go to Father's room at the end of the hallway because Father wanted to speak to James privately.

"James, I've known from the time you entered this school as a freshman you wanted to become a priest," Father Watson said. "Do you still want to be a priest?"

James nodded. "Yes, Father. I do."

Father Watson: "James, while being a homosexual doesn't necessarily prevent you from becoming a priest if you can keep it a secret, conduct like this is certainly unacceptable. If it becomes known a candidate for the seminary is homosexual, he will not be accepted."

"Yes, Father. I know," James said. "It's just this retreat has brought out feelings in me I didn't even know existed. Being alone with another boy for five nights—well, it was more than I could bear."

"I realize temptation is often hard to resist," Father Watson said. As he spoke, he walked to the bed James was sitting on, sat down next to him, put his arm around his shoulder and started kissing him. James did not object to Father Watson's advances and, before long, the two were having sex. Father Watson spoke to James after their sexual encounter was over.

"James, many of us in the priesthood, including myself, are homosexuals. It's necessary for us to hide it from those who do not accept it. It doesn't affect our ability to be good priests. In fact, it probably makes us better priests. If you truly have the calling, don't let being a homosexual stand in the way of becoming a priest. There is so much of God's work that needs to be done and so much good you can do you shouldn't allow anything to stand in your way if you are willing to make the sacrifices to become a priest. We will keep this interlude our little secret and never speak of it again to each other or to anyone else."

"Yes, Father," James said. "I want more than ever to become a priest, since you have shown me being a priest and being homosexual aren't mutually exclusive. I will be forever grateful to you."

So, the two men made a pact to wipe from their minds, and forever erase, the memory of what had just

Confessions, Lies, and Secrets   *Stu Milisci*

taken place. Little did they realize at the time how intertwined theirs lives would become.

#

About the Author

Stu Milisci is a retired New York City Police Sergeant. He and his wife of 50 years are recent migrants to Indian Harbour Beach, Florida. They have two adult children and five grandchildren ranging in age from 10 to 20.

He is a graduate of an all-boys Jesuit high school in Brooklyn, New York. In his capacity as a teenage student and as an adult law enforcement officer, he personally witnessed things and heard allegations which weren't able to be proven. These events made him aware of sexual abuse committed by members of the Catholic clergy. Unable to substantiate any of these allegations, he decided to write a novel dealing with this topic.

Stu Milisci
Indian Harbour Beach, FL

Confessions, Lies, and Secrets   *Stu Milisci*